To Emma, for believing in me when I didn't.

This book is a work of fiction. The characters, incidents, and dialog are products of the author's imagination, and any resemblance to actual events or persons, living or dead, is coincidental.

Copyright © 2015 Alex Davis
Published by Tickety Boo Press
www.ticketyboopress.co.uk

Cover Art by Gary Compton
Book Design by Big River Press Ltd

Other Space Opera books by
Tickety Boo Press

Endeavour – A Sleeping Gods Novel by Ralph Kern

Abendau's Heir by Jo Zebedee

A Prospect of War by Ian Sales

To Sue
Enjoy!!
A Davis

Prologue - A Birth in the Stars

Sejurus had grown used to many things about space. He was accustomed to the faint and endless sensation of movement around him, the limited chance to converse with his fellows, the hours of scientific analysis and research required of him.

The one thing he had never grown used to was the *darkness*.

Broken only be the intermittent light of distant stars, the shadows enveloped everything beyond the harsh glare of the ship. On the whole, he preferred not to look beyond the viewscreen, being much more comfortable in the small confines of his quarters or studying within his laboratory. But this was a momentous occasion, and one that he was determined not to miss.

Hiss.

Whoosh.

The sound had become familiar, but he had never *cared* about the cargo like this before. Creeping into view, sending blazing contrails into the infinite dark, went the phalanx of seeding pods. He tried to count them, but quickly lost track as they made their way towards the surface of the virgin planet.

Within their metallic flesh lay the core of new life, the beginnings of a race previously unseen to the universe. Sejurus had been involved from the very earliest days of this burgeoning experiment, and now he would finally see his efforts bear fruit. By now the seeding pods had disappeared so far into the distance that they must be breaking the atmosphere, preparing for descent and landing.

And dispersal.

'Sad to see them go, Sejurus?'

The voice from behind him is bold and clear. The voice of a leader, and one who had earned that title many times over.

'Sad is the wrong word, Canturus. It is a... mixture of emotions.'

'I hope that none of them are negative, Sejurus. You should be most proud of your work.'

'It is too soon to start swelling with pride. There is no knowing yet if this experiment will be a success.'

'The measure of success is to create life, Sejurus. What that life decides to do once we have seeded it... well, that is beyond our control.'

'Perhaps. The pressure here is...'

'Greater than anywhere else? Of course it is. That is precisely why you were chosen. You are one of the most intelligent among us, an intellectual titan among mental giants.'

'I appreciate your words, Canturus. They mean much coming from you.'

'Do not speak to placate me. I would like to know what troubles you.'

Sejurus turns to face Canturus for the first time. His superior is dressed simply, a marker of both modesty and confidence. To look at them, you could consider them equals, but nothing could be further from the truth. Canturus's authority does not come from trinkets or garments, but emerges from within him.

'What troubles me is how much lies at stake on this new race. What goes on here will determine much of not only our own future, but perhaps what lies ahead for all Ensium.'

'Of course.'

'What if... what if I have made some fatal miscalculation? An error in my workings?'

'I have the greatest of belief in you, my friend. I doubt that any such thing has happened.'

'Even if it has not, even if all the equations were perfect, what of it? The seeding pods will already have landed on the surface. As we speak, the simplest forms of life will be vented from the pods. The evolution will be starting shortly, and ending soon enough. That is when the imponderables begin!'

'Why do you worry about things beyond your control? Your role is complete - you have given them every chance to take the right path, to be the greatest of the races that we have birthed.'

'But what if they do not, Canturus? So much will be lost!'

'Nothing will be lost. All that we can do in this venture is *gain*. We may have to begin again, and we are not afraid to do so. If that time comes - and I hope it does not - you will once again be the man to lead the efforts.'

'After such a failure?'

'Failure is much of what enables us to learn. We have learned many lessons in our time, and no doubt there will be many more to come. The wise seek to avoid repeating these errors again. To fail does not make you a *failure*.'

Sejurus turns away from his ally, his disagreement tacit. Canturus steps alongside him, his eyes seeing the same darkness. The Animex have always sought to bring light to these shadowy wastes.

'Would you stay, Sejurus? Would you watch over them as a custodian, a guardian?'

'Given the choice? Yes, I would.'

'They are not your children, old friend. Admittedly you are their creator, but they are no part of you.'

'I do not seek to care for them. I feel... I feel like my work is not complete until they have settled, until I have *seen* them grow. What I have done so far is worth no acclaim.'

'If I could give you the chance to stay?'

'Down there? On Noukaria?'

'Ha! I have told you already you are not their father. They do not *need* you there. It is imperative we let them develop their own way. But... perhaps I could spare you a vessel?'

'You can do such a thing?'

'I can do much, Sejurus. Admittedly, it is an unusual request. But there may be value in it. There is much yet to discuss, of course. Such a decision cannot be made lightly. It would mean the loss of a great mind, but of course you would not remain here permanently.'

'No, I merely wish to see them on the right path.'

'Very well. I shall take it to the Council. Until then, you are welcome to remain here. The first days of the Noukari, eh, my friend?'

'Thank you, Canturus. I shall not forget what you have done for me.'

'It is not done yet. Take a moment here before getting back to your duties – there is much recording yet to be done.'

Sejurus nods, looking once more down at the sphere of Noukaria, wondering what the life he has placed there will bring.

THE BOOK OF APIUS

Apius sits at his simply constructed table, a sheet of papyrus laid before him. He smiles at the simplicity of what lays before him, a triumph in its own way. Just sunups ago no such thing existed, and now it is here before him.

At this very table, he shall create. He will create the book that will guide his race forwards.

Slowly, tentatively, he reaches for his quill, dips the end into the ink with a flourish and writes his first words.

The Noukari are the closest to holiness, the closest to purity. From the very heart and mind of the Animex they rose, the simplest of life-forms, born into the wilderness. But quickly they grew, and quickly they learned. The primordial gave way to the civilised, to the learned, to a growing intellect and society. The mastery of the distant gods

Apius pauses at his first use of this word. Gods. A defining moment in this ode to the Animex. Despite his momentary hesitation, the word feels right to him. Creators, those who gave life.

Gods.

The mastery of the distant gods made it so. In their sacred vessels the Noukari arrived, broken down to its simplest form. By the hands of the Animex we were crafted to resemble a God in both physical and mental form.

Apius places down the quill, the ink already beginning to run dry. Yes, that will suffice as a start. He knows that his words must be carefully chosen, and it will not pay to commit too much to the page at once. Satisfied, he places the scrawled page carefully to one side.

***

Across the settlement, known among its people as *Genem*, there is a welter of activity. The streets that intersect the huts see many at their designated duties in developing the settlement further. The activity is slow, steady in the stifling heat of the sun. Its denizens take on their duties willingly, knowing that each of them has a key role to play.

Just outside the town, there is a new vision coming slowly to completion. The jungles of Noukaria have been cut back further and further, making way for the new inhabitants of this planet. The Noukari call it their own, interlopers in a place that was once untamed.

The boundaries of this new construction stretch wide, and on two sides wooden walls are almost constructed. They reach almost half a mile already, but have yet to reach their apex. At the heart of this semi-complete building ten pale and tall figures move. Some of them work carrying wood, shifting planks to where they are needed. Elsewhere Noukari can be seen mixing *Adipus,* a soft substance from the *Astipo* plant that hardens once applied to any substance. Before its discovery, the Noukari lived in the simplest of huts and shelters, taking cover from the brutal heat and thunderstorms as best they could. Now the homes and huts of Genem are better equipped to deal with the conditions the jungles can offer.

Apius sees all of this from the edge of the settlement, watching his loyal followers as they edge closer to their mighty goal. The ultimate symbol of the power of the Gods!

The Temple of the Animex.

'How goes it, brothers?' he says as he emerges into the clearing. Immediately the building process stops as his followers blink, wide-eyed, at the sight of him. Apius waves away their amazement.

'Do not let me stop your important work. I wish only to speak with Viarus.'

Uncertainly, young and old return to their construction and Viarus leaves the shell of the temple. He attempts a bow, which is also waved away.

'Please, Viarus. I have told you not to bow.'

'My apologies, Apius.'

'How goes the temple? Are things on schedule?'

'I believe so.'

'Excellent. We shall hold a ceremony four sunups from now.'

'A ceremony, Apius?'

'Such a thing would only be fitting. To mark not only the completion of this temple, but the gods who put us here.'

'Gods?'

'Yes, Viarus. You have a problem with this word?'

'Of course not. In fact, I am pleased to hear you use it.'

'Why should that be so?'

'We talk. In fact, it is something we have much discussed. We spoke just this morning of whether the Animex were truly gods.'

'Interesting. What did you conclude?'

'That it was the only logical answer.'

Apius smiles. Placing a hand on Viarus's shoulder, he says, 'I am glad you and I agree on this. I will tell you something, Viarus. But I should like to tell you in confidence.'

'Of course.'

'Today I have undertaken a great venture, perhaps the equal of this temple. I have started to write a book, a volume to tell of the power of the Animex and the early days of our race, their children.'

'Such a book sounds... remarkable.'

'I believe it will be so. A chronicle, something we can pass to our children and they to theirs. But there is of course much to be done. The time will come for everyone to know, but that must wait.'

'I shall guard the secret with my life.'

'I know, Viarus. Now, I shall let you return to work.'

As Apius turns to leave, Viarus speaks again, summoning him back.

'There is one more thing, Apius.'

'Of course, brother.'

'We have been speaking much of... religious matters of late. You have led us in this path, showed us the way, been the guiding hand behind this construct.'

'I do only as I see necessary.'

'Modesty does not suit you, Apius. So many times you have proven yourself to be... something more than us. You speak, and we follow.'

'Your faith compels you, Viarus.'

'Faith is wasted if there is no-one to lead that belief. We should like to bestow you with a title.'

'A title? That is rather contrary to how our society functions.'

'Perhaps, but it would befit what you mean to us.'

'And what did you have in mind?'

'We would dub you *Re'Nuck*. He who communicates with gods.'

'I had never considered myself the holder of any position, brother.'

'Will you accept this title?'

'If you wish to address me as such, I shall consider it to the highest of honours.'

'Thank you, *Re'Nuck*.'

Apius smiles warmly before leaving Viarus to his task.

***

Once back within the confines of his simple hut, Apius considers the name. Re'Nuck. *He who communicates with the gods.* Perhaps he is not worthy of such a title, for the Animex have never spoken directly *to* him. And none of this fellow Noukari carry a title – he will be the first to rise above the equality of their society. Even those greatest experts in every respect hold no position, no marker of power.

But perhaps there is more to the moniker than that. Could it be that the Animex have somehow chosen to communicate *through* him, making him the instrument of their will? Apius is sharply aware of the importance of these early days of their existence, the vital impact they will have on the development of their society. He sees his responsibilities, and seeks to carry them out each day.

With that in mind, he takes up his quill once more and begins to write.

THE TEMPLE RISES

In Genem, there is little to life but survival. The Noukari are a new race growing used to life in their previously undisturbed home. At first, they lived in harmony with the planet, but as their intelligence and vision have grown they have sought to create ways to make their lives easier. Homes have sprouted seemingly from the ground, made from the solid wood of the trees around them. Paths allow citizens to wander freely from one place to the next. More buildings are coming along – social spaces, places of study. There is much pride at the development of Genem among a township that remembers with shame its earliest days.

Genem is a place with no absolute ruler – there are a few individuals who are looked up to as the wisest in certain respects. Among the builders, Exolos oversees and dispenses sage advice. When it comes to hunting, Lerusus offers his expertise and indeed his physical prowess to ensure success. In the fields, Ajerus watches over the crops with eyes that see more than the rest of the Noukari. But they have no true power – they are figureheads, nothing more. The Noukari have no true concept of power, or hierarchy. Each is content with their lot.

Among its people, each works in his or her own simple way – growing plants with a range of uses from food to medicine, hunting the more placid life in the forests of Noukaria, the Saren and the Lichuk and the Vopal, building houses, homes and communal establishments. Everyone strives to make it from one day to another, without any higher goal other than the completion of duty.

But something is changing within Genem. Many can see it, and some are willing to invest their time and their hearts in it.

The Temple of the Animex is now a swarm of activity, with fifty of the pale denizens of the village working feverishly towards its completion. Viarus stands on the ground as his fellows climb unsteady constructs of twig and branch, doing his best to direct the process in a manner to please the Re'Nuck.

Viarus takes a brief look away from the burgeoning temple to look at Apius, standing at the entrance to the clearing. His voice is lost beneath the din of chatter and construction, but before the Re'Nuck stands a crowd of thirty or more Noukari. The last twelve sunups have seen an incredible shift in feeling within Genem. Once Viarus had felt like an outsider because of his beliefs, but now many have flocked to become followers of the Re'Nuck. Viarus takes a little pride in creating the title that Apius now fills so admirably. The honorific has given Apius a new confidence, planted the final seeds of belief in his cause. And it is a belief that has become irresistible to many. As the sunups have passed, Viarus has found himself managing more workers, more labourers wanting to see the temple completed and willing to lend their energies. His role as overseer of the temple has grown into one that now takes up almost all his time, to the point that he has now started to sleep beneath the stars in the ever-expanding foundations of the temple. Even Exolos could not have done a better job.

Given the newfound workforce at his disposal, the temple may even be completed ahead of schedule. He turns from the Re'Nuck, refocussing his attention to the magnificent task ahead.

***

Outside the temple, whose two walls have grown to four, a proud and lyrical voice carries across the clearing. Beneath the spell of its powerful tones a loose congregation has gathered, without seats, without rows, without any location worthy of such worship.

No matter, the Re'Nuck thinks. *All of that will come in time.*

He does not allow this simple thought to interrupt the

rhythm of his speech. He has become expert in such matters – the words of the Book seem to have ingrained themselves into his memories, written there as large as they are on the crinkled pages at his hut.

'And the Noukari arrived, borne within the sacred vessels crafted by the gods themselves. But those simplest of lifeforms did not resemble us as we are today. Yet by the powers and craftsmanship of the Animex, we were able to rise from the simplest of forms to something more. It was within sunups that we first came to walk, to think, to speak.'

Apius pauses for a few seconds, taking a look at the rapt faces before continuing.

'We know all this to be fact. All of these things are burned into our common history, and live within our memories still. There is nothing I have said to be disputed. But the question that some still ask is what this truly means for our people. What interpretations can we offer for this event? In this respect we talk about the beginning of life, an act of creation beyond any we have encountered. We are their people, and Genem – and all of Noukaria – is every bit as much theirs as it as ours.'

The crowd nods thoughtfully. Apius has swiftly become used to these public appearances, and the necessary flourishes of the spiritual leader. The means to instil his belief, to communicate in the name of the gods.

'No act of nature nor of building can do such a thing. It is clear that we were made by the hand of gods – gods called the Animex! There is no other conclusion, and in time all of those who have yet to accept will come to believe. Rest assured, those in denial shall soon worship with us. And they will share the word in a temple that surely even the gods cannot deny, a building so grand in scale that it would be worthy for a god to set foot within.'

Apius bows his head for a moment, allowing his newly-embroidered robe to billow around him. The new vestment has come with the title, and sets him apart from those who hang to his words.

'That is all. Go with these words, and spread them in the

streets and fields of Genem. Much has been done, but there is a longer road ahead.'

One by one the followers of Apius drift away, carrying eager conversations with them.

'Re'Nuck!'

The voice of Viarus echoes across the clearing, and Apius sees his closest companion waving him over. Apius is happy to comply.

'What do you think, Re'Nuck?'

'Recent progress has been remarkable, brother. Well done.'

'More come each sunup. You *bring* more here.'

Apius takes a moment to appreciate his own design, which is now finally approaching a kind of life. Perhaps this is something of the joy the Animex felt in their creation, a small spark of the divine.

'They come because of the truth, brother. How far are we from completion?'

'At this rate? Mere sunups, Re'Nuck.'

'Wonderful. The exterior is spectacular, but that is worth nothing if within lies a hovel. I must consider the inner decorations, ensure that it fits the grandeur our gods themselves would expect.'

'I see. Such a thing should not take long, given the right workers and skills.'

'I shall work on the designs overnight. Be ready to begin on sunup.'

'Yes, my Re'Nuck.'

***

The village of Genem, in itself, is a simple enough thing. A conglomeration of huts, built from wood harvested from the trees of the forest that surrounds them, bound together with the Adipus that is leeched from their bark. Their roofs are constructed with branch and vine, enough to keep out the hard rains that fall towards and sometimes beyond sundown.

Simple enough, perhaps, if it had not appeared on the

surface of Noukaria barely a human month before. To the natural order of the planet it has emerged like a boil. To the Noukari it has become a bastion of hope after those earliest days of desperate shelter beneath fallen trees and hollow logs. Apius remembers those times with a shudder as he walks the pathways of the settlement, although he recalls those primal sunups through a lens of experience and wisdom, the intellect that now exists within their race nowhere to be found at that time.

It is generally unheard of for a civilised creature to be able to look back so sharply at its primitive form. The collective memory sits like a scar on each of them. Clambering up the trees and sleeping on branches, chasing down defenceless animals to chew on their raw meat, scampering away in fear from rain and lightning...

We were beasts. But we evolved, and evolved so quickly.

Apius has become aware of the glances that he has begun to attract from those living within Genem. Those he knows look upon him with reverence, acknowledging him with a bow or other prostration. These he responds to with simple platitudes, blessings in the name of the Animex, furthering belief with each word.

But there are still many within Genem who have yet to accept, and to them his robed figure brings equal measures of suspicion and hatred. They do not yet recognise his position, and the influence it brings. He is not blind to the sideways glances, the baleful eyes, the naked curiosity that surrounds him. But he knows that he needs this as much as he needs his followers. Curiosity leads to questions, and questions to answers.

And there is only one answer they can reach.

What is it about him that inspires this reaction, he wonders? Is it his manner, his confidence, the doubtlessness of his belief? The fine robe he wears, woven from the fur of the rare Pilur, separating him from the multitudes? The staff he bears, fashioned into the shape of a wooden sceptre?

'Re'Nuck!'

The greeting disturbs his train of thought, and he sees an eager and pallid figure striding in his direction. The lady bows before him, but her eyes stare into Apius's own in a manner he finds disconcerting. The stare is fixed, unwavering. He can sense her eyes questing, silently asking something of him. He does not break the moment, but looks back with equal intensity. Finally her eyes separate from his, and she looks across at what he assumes to be her home.

'Yes, my sister?'

'I have heard much of your words, and wanted to speak to you.'

'Of course. You have questions for me?'

'Yes, many questions.'

'I shall be pleased to hear them, sister.'

'Good.' She rises to her full height, any obsequence now evaporated. 'Why do you build a temple?'

'Why? Such a simple question. We build it as a place to worship,' he replies.

'That is not what I mean. I wish to know what justification you have.'

'Justification?'

'The question is clear, *brother*.' She spits this last, no longer conceding to his rank. 'There is much to do here in Genem. The people live in ramshackle huts while you greedily stockpile wood and Adipus for your grand temple.'

'Greedily? Rest assured, sister, there is no greed involved. The temple is not to be my home!'

'It is not being built for me, nor my *Hasban*. It is not being constructed for our neighbours. It is an indulgence for you and the *cult* you are gathering around you.'

'Cult? It is no such thing. I simply look to spread the word of the Animex. What people take from them is their own choice.'

'They are your own words, *Re'Nuck*. Remember that. If the Animex are so powerful, I have no doubt they would speak for themselves.'

With her piece said, the woman heads back to her rustic home, her Hasban ushering her across the threshold. She spits on the floor in Apius's direction before heading into the residence.

Shaken, Apius heads back to his own hut with all the

dignity he can muster. His only relief is that there were few present to see the outburst.

INSIDE FOUR WALLS

Zerial watches his Wefi enter their home, the tension still too evident in her pinched expression. She strides to face the wall, not looking at her Hasban Zerial approaches, placing a hand on her shoulder, which is brushed off indelicately.

'I wish you hadn't done that, Asha.'

Asha spins quickly to face him. The tears in her eyes may be impotent fury, or something else.

'It needed to be done. Too many have kowtowed to him.'

'I agree. But in the public view is neither time nor place to say it!'

'Where is better? Apius wants to do everything in public view. He speaks in public view. He builds his blasted temple in public view. He blesses his followers in public view.'

'So you see fit to lower yourself to his level?'

'Lower myself? I would never descend to that. My concern is with *everybody*, Zerial. Unlike the *Re'Nuck*.'

'I know that, Asha. Your heart is good, anyone would say so.'

'So you know why I had to do that. I will not allow him to continue on his path, Hasban'

'But why must it be our business? There are *hundreds* here in Genem. Why must you be the one to lead this fight?'

'Because no-one else has found the courage to do so! Someone, somewhere should have told Apius what he needed to hear. With everyone else cowering - including *you* - it has fallen to me.'

'You accuse me of cowering? I do no such thing!'

'Why did you stand by here in the doorway, doing nothing?'

'I do not have to justify myself.'

'Perhaps you do.'

'I am not going to have this discussion, Asha. You went too far today.'

'Time will tell. You are in denial every bit as much as the *Re'Nuck's* deluded followers.'

Asha does not wait for a reply before she leaves the hut.

***

The next sunup, Apius arrives to the clearing to see that his temple has taken another vast step forward. The sight soothes the worries of yesterday's confrontation and the uneasy night that followed. For a moment he cannot understand how such a thing is possible, but when he looks more closely he can see the reason why. The breaking light reveals Noukari climbing and moving in a whirl of activity. Viarus notices Apius at the verge of the clearing and dashes to greet him. There are dark circles under his eyes, but tiredness does not have him beaten yet. His most loyal follower looks full of nervous energy, fighting exhaustion with raw excitement.

'What do you think, Re'Nuck?'

'You have outdone yourself, Viarus. How is all of this possible?'

'Everyone has gathered together, in a manner I have never seen before. We have been here all night, without rest or pause. Everyone wants to see the temple completed, and begin worshipping there.'

'Well, this is remarkable work. Thank you, Viarus. Your dedication gives me even further strength.'

'Do you have the designs for the interior, Re'Nuck?'

'I am afraid I do not, Viarus. Last night was... not easy for me.'

'How so, Re'Nuck?'

'It does not matter. I shall bring the designs this sundown. When will the exterior be complete?'

'At our present rate? The next sunup should see things completed fully.'

'Do your workers not need to sleep?'

'They will sleep when this is done, and rest proudly after their accomplishments.'

'Thank you, Viarus.'

***

From beyond the fringe of the clearing, Asha watches as the crowds gather. She is surprised to see so many familiar faces from around Genem. There are even a few of her co-workers on the fields, people who will in due course be headed to the plantations in a bid to grow reliable food, food that can be more easily attained. Living from plants growing in the hearts of the forest cannot be sustained in the long term, but with her colleagues so distracted, will anything be achieved? She marvels at the numbers continuing to arrive, now gathering to a throng of past fifty. Some have arrived on their own, looking uncertain as to what they are doing there – they are soon heartily welcomed. Many arrive in larger groups, talking animatedly about what is to come. What is it that this Re'Nuck offers, Asha wonders, that they need so desperately? What drags them from their homes so early in the day to hear one individual speak?

The Re'Nuck right now stands alone, ostracising himself in the manner of someone *above* all of those around him. Asha did not know Apius before all of this, but he was not whispered of as anything remarkable. She has been unable to find out where the name came from, but knows its resonance lies at the heart of this assembly. Re'Nuck. *He who communicates with the gods.*

Nonsense, she thinks to herself. Lifting himself above the rest of their number in such a manner!

Even from her distant vantage, she can hear the words of Apius as he turns dramatically and begins his speech. The voice carries with the essence of an echo as Apius projects each syllable.

'Good sunup, brothers and sisters. And this is a glorious

sunup indeed. You see before you the progress being made in the construction of the Temple of the Animex. This has been made possible by belief, by the faith and the dedication given by you and those like you. Tirelessly, the brothers and sisters of our religion have devoted their entire night to continuing construction. Led by my finest brother, Viarus, and lit only by the moons above us, they have not even let the sundown cease their endeavours! What you see before you is not a miracle, merely an affirmation that anything can be achieved when it is done in the name of the Animex!'

A roar of approval rises from the crowd, ringing out so loudly that Asha does not notice the presence approaching from behind her. When Zerial reaches out to touch her shoulder, Asha starts.

'Calm down, Wefi! It is I!'

'Hasban! What are you doing here?'

'I could ask you that question, Asha. Jupos said you had not yet arrived at the fields.'

'What of it? I am not alone in that.' She points outwards at the congregation.

'Of course you are not alone in that. The followers of the Re'Nuck have asked Ajerus for special permission to both arrive and depart late. Which is more than I can say for you.'

'Ajerus will understand.'

'Perhaps. You know he is a hard taskmaster. Why are you here rather than performing your duties?'

'I wanted to find out what this was all about. I have heard much, but... never witnessed it myself.'

'And what do you think, now you have seen it?'

'I think Apius uses too many words.'

'That is all you have to complain about? His verbosity?'

'I do not mean that. He speaks much of matters he knows little about. He has no more knowledge than you or I.'

'They are looking for guidance, Asha. You can hardly hold such a thing against them.'

'Are you with him, Zerial? Are you one of his followers also?'

'Of course not.'

'You speak like one, Hasban Every time I attack his motives and his actions, you leap to his defence.'

'I simply do not...' Zerial pauses, clutching for the words.

'Do not *what*?' Asha's level stare forces him to continue.

'I do not wish to see you involved in this. Confrontations in the street? Haunting the shadows? This is not the behaviour of the Asha I know.'

'Then perhaps you do not know me that well, Hasban'

'Why is this *your* crusade, Wefi?'

'If you have to ask, it shows how little you understand.'

Zerial shakes his head, this time unable to find any words. It is Asha who breaks the uneasy silence.

'I have seen enough. I should get to the fields.'

Asha nods before rustling away into the light forest around the clearing. Zerial watches her go, choosing to take the more familiar pathway back to Genem.

***

As good as his word, Apius returns to the Temple of the Animex next sunup with papyrus in his hands. The work on the designs was more rushed than he would have liked, but he is pleased to have it completed. Much of the work already existed within his mind. The act of drawing them was merely a final step.

When he reaches close enough to the temple to see it clearly, he is forced to pause in his tracks. The hordes of workers are now gone from it, and only a few people move around the exterior now. But that is because the outer aspects of the temple are *finished*. Apius looks upward in amazement at the vast scale of the walls, the dizzying heights of the spired chimney, the finely smoothed wood of the outside surface. Taking his final steps reverently, he touches the temple with both hands, just to reassure himself it is real. The physicality of the wall beneath his hands confirms it is the truth.

'The gods are welcome here,' he whispers to himself.

'As are you, Re'Nuck.' The voice of Viarus intrudes into what Apius had thought was a private moment, but is not unwelcome.

'Brother, this is exceptional... I could weep at the very sight of it.'

'It is only the reality of your designs, Re'Nuck.'

'You do yourself much injustice, brother. What I did was draw my vision, the very simplest part of this process. You have gathered materials, men and women, ensure that the construction did not collapse or crumble...'

'There was little chance of that, with your vision behind it.'

'Vision is one thing, Viarus. Even someone with vision needs the right people around him, those who can make visions come true. You have proven yourself to be more than able in that respect. Thank you, Viarus.'

'No thanks are needed, Re'Nuck. We do it for you and for the Animex with a willing heart.'

'Your modesty does you proud, brother.'

'Would you like to look inside, Re'Nuck?'

'I should like nothing more.'

Viarus smiles, swings open the ornate door, and invites the Re'Nuck into the building. Apius takes his first steps steadily, wanting to savour the moment rather than devour it, drinking in the sight of the temple.

'The Temple of the Animex,' he breathes to himself. Craning to stare upwards, he can see the walls tapering, reaching towards the pinnacle of the temple, the spire with its simple chimney. It will serve as a release for the oils and perfumes Apius intends to burn. The walls on the inside are just as smooth as those on the exterior, and the Re'Nuck marvels at the care that has been paid to the whole building. With so many working on it, there seems to have been no single item of his design missed. He breathes in the smell of fresh-cut wood, the cleanliness of the earth beneath the floors, the uninhabitedness of the place. Soon it will be filled with worshippers, a proper and worthy place for the word of the Animex to be heard.

'Inside these four walls, we can truly begin.'

The Work of the Earth

Asha arrives early to the fields, determined to make up for yestersunup's late appearance. Ajerus did no more than insist she stay later to make up the lost time, something she had intended to do anyway. She hopes that her additional efforts this morning will be enough for that to be forgotten. She begins raking the rows of seeds, which stretch as far as the eye can see. Many trees had to be cleared to make way for this cropland, but the wood from those has provided the raw products to make many homes within Genem.

Asha shakes her head as she wonders how much forest was levelled to allow Apius his temple.

Ajerus arrives not long after her, giving her a gentle wave. 'Keen to start today, Asha?'

'I believe it was important to make up for yestersunup.'

'A good attitude. That I have never questioned.'

'I am glad to hear it.'

'Is there any sign of growth in this quadrant?'

'Nothing yet.'

'Hmm. Perhaps it remains too soon.'

'It is impossible to know. That is why we are taking on this task, is it not?'

'How do you mean?'

'You may have the others fooled, Ajerus, but not me. This whole venture is purely an experiment.'

'The effort here is to provide more food for Genem.'

'Of course, on one level. But if you know so much about how the crops grow, why do we have so many different crops in so many different fields?'

'Do you want to eat the same meal each sunup, each sundown? We require *variety*.'

'Nonsense. The first priority for you is to see what will grow, and how quickly it will do so, and in what amounts. Then you will refine what will be grown.'

Ajerus turns away, looking out over the vast swathes of land which hold the hope for their future. It is rare to see them as quiet as they are now.

'Did you only come early to have this conversation with me?'

'Just a happy accident.'

'Very well, I am sick of having to keep such a secret. All of your colleagues believe I know what I am doing, that I am somehow *in tune* with the earth. None of that is true.'

'It does not matter to me.'

Ajerus turns back to face her.

'What? Then why do you even bring this up?'

'I wanted my suspicions confirmed. I think no less of you. You do a fine job, and are well respected.'

'That respect is founded on a lie.'

'Do not kid yourself, Ajerus. There are many lies around us. Some necessary, some not.'

Like the denial of this gift?

Asha is stunned by Ajerus's use of the mental speech, something that many know exist but has rarely been acknowledged this way.

I do not know if that is a lie, Ajerus. Perhaps just a necessity.

Perhaps.

'I am glad we had this conversation, Ajerus. It is good to know the truth of this matter. I shall work just as hard to make sure we achieve our aims.'

'Will you tell the others of this?'

'Of course not. It is irrelevant to me, and I cannot see what good sharing this information will do.'

'Thank you, Asha. If you'll excuse me, I have much work to prepare.'

'Of course.'

***

Asha watches the remainder of her colleagues arrive. The talk, when she finally has some company, is only of one thing – The Temple of the Animex. She listens intently, although holds her tongue for now. There is much surprise that the construction is complete, and there is also some debate about the merits of the burgeoning religion. Hilius seems sold on the hypnotic words of Apius, and is delighted that he and his fellows now have a building in which to hear the sermons. Jupos is far less convinced, and doesn't want to hear anything about the Animex. Her attitude is very much one of keeping your head down, although Hilius thinks she is denying a significant issue. Jupos responds by saying that the most significant issue is the ground beneath her feet. Her third companion, Deriz, has decided to head to the temple to see if this new religion is for him. He is undecided, and joins little in the conversation, preferring to find out more from Hilius. The four of them work watering their dedicated patch of land, turning the soil and looking closely for signs of growth from beneath. These seeds have been entitled *Paluri,* a fruit which to date has only been found deep in the forests.

'What do you think, Asha?' asks Jupos.

'Hmm?'

'About the matter of the Re'Nuck?'

'Apius?'

'You don't like his title?' interjects Hilius.

'I don't see what he has done to earn it. He seemed to simply turn up with it one day.'

'The Re'Nuck earns the title every day!' Hilius's voice is raised, and in her peripheral vision Asha can see both Jupos and Deriz moving towards the other side of their quadrant.

Cowards. Afraid of the faintest confrontation.

'In what way, Hilius? By standing and shouting in front of a crowd? I could do the same, if I chose.'

'The Re'Nuck did not choose to do so, he *was* chosen!'

'You become defensive too quickly, Hilius. You can shout and cry all you like, but there is doubt underneath your words.'

'Doubt? The Re'Nuck is a great leader, just the kind of person that Genem needs.'

'That Genem *needs*? Who are you to decide what Genem needs? We have never had titles and leaders before. There are more pressing matters at hand that praising the "gods".'

'You side with Jupos, then?'

'In essence, yes. But Jupos's views are milder than mine, rest assured. I look at all the effort that has gone towards that temple and cry to think what else could have been done. These fields could be twice the size, growing the food we need. They could have been out in the forests, hunting for food to sustain us. There are still many buildings needed around Genem, and the materials that could have built them is now invested in a temple!'

'Your vision is so short, Asha. The food and the buildings will take care of themselves, in time. But for now what we need most of all is to ensure we set off on the right spiritual path!'

'At least we can agree on that. But I would rather have food in my belly than a contented soul.'

'Then you are sorely misguided, Asha. Belief will take care of much.'

'Work and integrity will take care of much.'

'Now you question the Re'Nuck's *integrity*?'

'What evidence have you of his integrity? What makes you think he communicates with the gods?'

Hilius steps forward, his stance tense and coiled. The wooden hoe is raised in his hands, as though he were ready to strike out.

'You are wrong. You cannot see it, but you are wrong. And in time you will come to know it.'

'We shall see just how far your idolatry gets you, Hilius.'

Hilius throws down his hoe and turns away, stomping furiously away from the quadrant.

***

On the opposite side of Genem, in a field untouched by agriculture but trampled by the many feet of a procession, the temple rises gloriously into the sky, backlit by the orange sun. Even from outside, a booming voice can be heard – the certain tones of the Re'Nuck.

Within the temple, the decorations are still yet to be put in place. But that has not stopped many arriving to hear the word of the Animex, sitting on the floor or leaning against the walls. Each of them stares intently at the Re'Nuck, who does not stand at an altar or lectern as he had envisaged. Still, he knows he will remember this sermon, perhaps more than any other.

'A very warm welcome, all, to the Temple of the Animex! You may be thinking to yourself that this place looks basic. For now that is true. But as quickly as this magnificent building came to be, so will the interior of this temple realise a similar beauty. The first thing I wish to say today is thank you. When I first set out upon this path, all I had was belief, nothing more. I thought that if I could pass my belief to one person, that would be a success. To be stood here feels like a wonderful dream. And it is all of you that have made that so. With your faith in the Animex, with your dedication, with your efforts and labour and generosity. So I thank each and every one of you for allowing me this moment.'

A cheer emerges from the crowd, and Apius allows them their moment. The sound resonates throughout the temple.

'Please, brothers and sisters, let us commence with sermon for today. This place is made for the worship of the Animex, our fathers and creators.'

Apius pauses. No-one dares break this moment. It seems as though the congregation is unwilling to even *breathe*.

'Genem has grown swiftly around us, and it will be the first of many settlements, you can rest assured. As we, the Noukari, move forward, there will be more. Perhaps this will be the largest – perhaps this will be dwarfed by those that will come in time. We must strive to be great, because in this respect we are the closest thing to the gods! We must tread the footsteps they once trod, guiding a new society in the proper direction!'

A pause. Reverent silence. Apius can feel the temple amplifying his words in a way that is both physical and emotional. Imagine it full to the brim with finery and regalia!

'So this is a time when we must all rise. And that process has already begun with the walls that surround you. But we must continue to ascend, to become greater than we are, greater than we have ever been. This is a time for the Noukari to truly assume the mantle of the children of the gods!'

With this final, booming proclamation, Apius allows the thunderous applause to ring out around him.

First Worship

Sunup comes quickly, almost too quickly for the two moons. Their pallid outlines can be seen in the sky above Noukaria, their luminescence drowned out by the orange glare of the sun. The village sees its denizens heading out on their appointed tasks. Fieldworkers rush to their respective quadrants, builders gather materials and carry them to their place of work, hunters collect their basic weaponry and say goodbye to their Wefis and Hasbans. It may be the last time they see them. For each placid Saren and Vopal, there remains the ever-present danger of the Hiyel. Each took on their role willingly in the early days of their gathering, before even the huts of Genem had been formed, and those roles remain many sunups on. Sacrifice and integrity is what Noukari civilisation has been based upon.

But this particular sunup sees many heading in one direction – towards a clearing at the edge of the village, and towards the vast building that swallows up so much of it. They carry crudely lashed chairs, simply woven silks, rudimentary carvings and offerings of whatever they consider valuable.

These provide merely a starting point.

Over the sunups that follow the items being lugged to the temple grow more elaborate and more wondrous. Their carriers beam with pride as they discuss what they have found or constructed with their fellow worshippers.

All the while, Asha watches them. The misplaced pride sickens her, as does the amount that Apius continues to ask while other tasks are ignored. She has heard the whispers on the field, where Hilius has refused to speak to her since their disagreement. He has been looking full of himself, filled with the gloatish pride that has possessed so many. Jupos has told her all she needs to know about the ceremony anyway.

Then Ajerus comes to inform her that she is being moved to another quadrant.

'What is this about, Ajerus? Why this sudden change?'

'It must be this way, Asha.'

'What does that mean? This is about Hilius, isn't it?'

Ajerus looks down at the ground, unwilling to answer.

'Well! Tell me, Ajerus. You are supposed to be the leader here, aren't you? If you can't bear to tell me the truth...'

Very well. It is about Hilius. But not just that.

Why the sudden change of speech, Ajerus? Afraid people might overhear?

Perhaps. They could probably overhear if they attempted to do so.

We don't know that.

It's not just because of Hilius. He and I... started to talk. About everything.

Everything? It is quite apparent to me that you mean only one thing.

Must you always be so direct?

Direct? I simply call it the truth.

Very well. Hilius spoke to me about the work of the Re'Nuck. I was curious, so I attended a sermon.

Sermons? Is that what he calls them?

Please, Asha. It just so happens that I was inspired by his vision.

What vision is that? Of him sat atop a throne, commanding Genem as though he was a god?

That's enough, Asha. My decision is made. You have a new quadrant, and a new set of co-workers.

You're moving me so I don't cause trouble.

If you must put it that way, yes. I don't want any more difficulties. What we have to do here is important enough.

So you waste time playing at religion!

Marshal yourself, Asha. I would hate to have to remove you from the workforce.

Yes, master. I shall go to my new quadrant at once. Enjoy all your religious discussion.

Asha...

She finds herself surprised that she can snap her mind closed so quickly. Ajerus looks at her, stunned, but she says nothing more before making her exit.

***

Half of Genem buzzes with an unfamiliar excitement. After short lives filled with work and drudgery and duty, there is the promise of celebration, something to break the routine strangling each sunup. The other half of the population are mystified, uncertain, a little curious. Perhaps some of them will attend, simply to see what this new religion might mean to them. It could be something life-changing. It may alter nothing. But it offers something different, a much-needed variety.

Asha watches people heading towards the temple from the doorway of her hut, shooting sullen stares at anyone who glances in her direction. Zerial sits uneasily, wishing his wefi would come back inside. It is as if she attempts to stop people from going to the temple by willpower alone, killing their excitement and sending them scurrying back to their huts. But people simply continue to file their way towards the temple.

'I can scarcely believe what I see, Zerial. So many I had considered to be good people. So many I had considered better than this.'

'Calm down, Asha. I doubt that all of them are true *believers*.'

'Does that make it better?'

'Well, they may not get swept up in it all.'

'*May* not. So we might be losing more to Apius.'

'In what sense are they lost to us, Wefi? They believe something you do not. Is that so irreparable?'

'It might be.'

'You have become such a doomsayer, Asha. With every word you seem to spout venom!.'

'Venom? Is that how you see me, Hasban?'

'That is what you are becoming. Where is the carefree Asha that I was paired with, the girl that ran through the forests and cried her joy to the moons?'

'That was a long time ago.'

'Not so long, my love. Not so many sunups we should lose count. Our race is not so old, Asha.'

'Very well. But much has happened since then.'

'Enough to leech all the happiness from you? Your character has begun to change so deeply, and I do not... I do not know how to recover you. I feel as though you are lost to me.'

'Then perhaps I am. Perhaps there is no way to recover what we have.'

Zerial sighs, having no recourse. The conversation was supposed to open some kind of channel between them, bring them closer, remind them of what it means to be Hasban and Wefi.

'Perhaps it does not mean what you think, Zerial.'

She walks out of the door as she says this, her footsteps crunching softly on the forest floor.

***

Asha blends into the crowds heading towards the ceremony. She attracts a glance or two, nothing more than would be expected. She feels self-conscious, as if people can sense that she is not one of them. She casts off the feeling, mixing with everyone as openly as she can. She is surprised by how naturally falsity comes to her. She returns empty words with her own neo-religious proclamations, and is able to pass as one of the flock. The only thing she is missing is the offering in her hands that most of them have. For a moment she sees Hilius in the crowd, but hangs back to avoid crossing his line of sight. It doesn't matter if she arrives as one of the last to the ceremony, as long as she is *there*. She has to see what this is about, and just what it will lead to.

She trails into the clearing as one of the last of a long procession, talking uneasily with those around her, masking her ignorance as to previous sermons. She hates to admit that the temple is a spectacular building. *Too* much so. How many of their number have slaved to create such a thing? Despite herself, she feels a slight chill as she enters the Temple of the Animex. The interior of the temple is sumptuously appointed, at least the part of it she can see. It seems as though almost all of Genem is crammed into this space to hear this. It is all she can do to angle herself a space at the rear of the temple. Craning her neck, she can see Apius stood before the congregation, placed behind a wooden altar festooned with plants and flowers. She recognises some of them as being rare, found far from Genem. What else will the Re'Nuck's vanity drive him to? The hubbub of the crowd dies down as Apius steps before the audience. A woman reaches out to him, but her hand is snatched back, presumably by a chastising Hasban

'My brothers, my sisters, welcome to this most auspicious of sundowns. The moons will bear witness to this, and the gods too shall behold our ceremony.'

The crowd surges forward, and Asha is glad that she chose her small space against the back wall. It looks as though people could get hurt, but no-one seems to consider it.

'This sundown shall henceforth be marked as one of our most significant. This we shall call First Worship, to recall the first time we gave praise to the gods on the completion of our temple!'

The dense audience bursts into a wall of noise, and Asha feels as though the sound is pressing against her with a physical force.

'This is the Temple of the Animex, and we are the Animexians! Embrace your new name as you embrace the words of your Re'Nuck, and the influence of the Animex in your own life!'

Apius revels in the roar of the audience, threatening to break into a frenzy. With a simple motion, the Re'Nuck brings them back to silence.

'We all know the facts of our arrival here. We arrived here in vessels crafted by the hands of the Animex, made to bring their children here safely. When we were young, we were mere animals. Since that day, each sunup we have become more advanced, and we have grown closer to their image. We share their wisdom, their intelligence. And from nothing we have crafted a society, and each of us has taken on a role to make that civilisation work. But our evolution is not yet complete.'

Asha has to admire his handiwork, the careful design behind his performance. And that is exactly what it is – a performance. How can a man like Apius truly believe that of which he speaks? The Animex made life, but does that make them gods? The Re'Nuck has found a language to control the villagers of Genem. Even in this simple pause he is fully in charge of everyone in this temple.

'The next step – the next phase for us – is to truly accept the Animex. Each one of us should devote out lives to them, to worshipping them with our acts and our prayers. For they hear us – do not doubt it. They watch over us, see our actions. Everything we have built they have watched us build. Every word we say they have heard us speak. So let us let them know. Let us make them understand how much we appreciate the gift of life they have given!'

Apius finally deigns to walk among the crowd, his people. They part before him, giving him the space to wander freely while they push into even smaller spaces. 'And we shall appreciate every moment this precious life gives us. Tonight we shall celebrate, and begin the *enjoyment* of these lives. We shall forget our duties, and our responsibilities, and lose ourselves in revelry!'

Asha is horrified at the thought, and that horror only intensifies as the flock crows its agreement. What Apius proposes is against everything Genem has been built upon!

'I bid you all to return to your huts, and bring all you can to this clearing! Bring instruments that we may play music until sunup! Bring food and drink that we may feast until we are full! Be ready to dance, and laugh, and enjoy starlit pleasures! Let the ceremony of First Worship *begin*!'

The temple begins to empty. People attempt to barge past each other in their enthusiasm. Asha curls herself into a ball, afraid of what she is seeing from her fellows. Is the potential for his behaviour in all of them, within her? Here in the corner she feels an element of safety, and as people depart the manic energy that has been built up leaves the temple, a change in the air beyond the chill of moontime. Asha feels unwilling to move until there is utter silence around her. She finally stands in the empty temple, unable to speak, unable to *understand* what she has just seen.

But the temple is not completely empty. Stood in the central aisle, draped in vestments, stands the Re'Nuck himself. He glances over to her, and she realises that this is the first time she has been alone with this man.

'What a surprise to see you. Not satisfied with bawling at me in the streets? Or have you finally decided to join us?'

'Join you? I shall have no part of... *this*.'

'Then why are you here? Just idle curiosity?'

'Of course not. I came to...' As the words linger on her lips, she realises how ridiculous they sound. But Apius is not willing to let them go.

'You came to *stop me*? Is that right, Asha?'

'How do you know my name?'

'It is quite easy enough to find out. Besides, it is worth knowing your opposition. I would not want to see my cause... damaged in any way.'

'You consider this a cause? This is a squandering of resources to vanity. Vanity and empty words!'

'You will see just how empty they are in time. Enough people have flocked here to the temple. Do you think they consider my words empty?'

'No, but their minds must be!'

'Asha, really? Judging so many of your fellows to be buffoons, just because they happen to believe in something more than what we can see? Something more than drowning in hardship?'

'So the answer is revelry? Feasting and games? What does that solve?'

'Do you truly think that any god would enjoy watching their children grow like this? Toiling away in fields over plants that have yet to sprout? Building a village that is little more than a circle of huts? Developing tools to make the same labour quicker? Is that a fit life for the children of *gods?*'

'What do you know of these gods, Apius? What makes you so wise in their ways? Have you seen the Animex, spoken with them, heard this from them?'

'I know what I say is true. I feel them smile upon me.'

'Your followers might swallow such nonsense, *Re'Nuck*, but I know what you are doing.'

Apius says the next with his mind, not with his tongue. But the touch of it... Ajerus's mental hand upon her was gentle, uninvasive. The words Apius places into her are scalding, each letter and syllable a burning brand.

You see nothing. It has already begun, and I will see it through to the end.

Asha reels backward, sighing with relief as the clutching mind-grip of Apius releases itself. Without another word, spoken or thought, she dashes from the temple.

***

Within hours, the clearing is witness to a scene unlike any in the short history of Genem. Larders have been emptied, and food lies on crude tables where both men and women eat greedily. None think about the next sunup. They eat as they have never eaten, gorging until their stomachs grow bloated. In one corner an unseen man has overstuffed himself more than any other, and vomits loudly into a stand of trees. Some of the food lies on the floor, trodden upon by bare feet, but still is devoured by hungry hands and mouths. 'Let us eat! Eat like we shall never eat again!' a high-pitched voice cries, and instantly the feeding frenzy intensifies.

But feasting is not the only act of pleasure evident around the temple. To one side a dancing circle has broken out, three women playing their simplest of drums with a fervour that sucks the crowd into a hypnotic rhythm. None of the Noukari have ever danced before, and the movements are jerky, often arrhythmic. Some find the beat to the music, other simply fling limbs and heads around with abandon, not caring what the music is but for the fact that there *is* music. The result is a swirling mass of bodies, some pressing against each other, others seeking isolation, their own space to explore the movement of their bodies. Each is lost in a new world, a world of sound and ecstasy.

Apius watches the dancers from the sidelines, choosing not to join them. He knows that he is the originator of this ceremony, but must not partake of it himself. No - a Re'Nuck must not debase himself like this. He has a duty to his followers. They must know this pleasure, they must find it at the heart of them to *forget* duty and endless work. This is significant, he knows, and he must take in every aspect of the sights before him without losing himself.

He leaves the dancers to their furious patterns, passes the desperate feeders at the centre of First Worship. For there is something more going on at the ceremony, something he had not expected.

At the outer edge of the clearing there is a small clutch of men, only four or five, but what they do is so extraordinary that he cannot help but watch.

They are *fighting*.

The Re'Nuck moves in more closely, and the offence and defence pauses for a moment. But Apius just nods and bids them to continue. None of them question further, and the slowest to respond to the Re'Nuck's command find their faces crushed with clenched fists.

Fighting, Apius thinks to himself. What an unlikely outcome. Only in this moment, freed of all their rules and strictures, have they seen fit to fight. He would not even recognise it had he not heard and seen the creatures of the forest doing the very same thing, from the small and clumsy Echen through to the vicious duels of the Hiyel. It seems to be the way of nature, he reflects, the way of all life. Perhaps there is even something unnatural in the fact they have *never* fought.

Do the Animex fight like this? Combat between god and

god, creators turned destroyers? Surely such a thing must be if their children have this capacity for conflict within them.

There seems to be no routine to the combat, no pattern. Who has ever thought to develop rules for this situation? The fight is not over pride, or honour. It is simply a fight because there is the *will* to fight. The five men - he counts them now - have no particular aggressor, but lash out at the nearest person to them. They seem to absorb the blows with fist and elbow with delight equal to the successful strikes they land. Causing pain - and feeling pain - seems to be their unique pleasure.

And perhaps something more.

Apius revels in the stunning scene, limbs twisting to punch and kick, throws launching bodies to the remorseless floor. He sees their grimaces as jaws are rocked by fists, and headbutts connect with crunching force, and sweat breaks out on exhausted faces. But still they do not stop. What could make them stop?

Under the moons, the Re'Nuck watches it all. He watches his people gorge, and revel, and fight.

First Worship has succeeded beyond his imaginings.

What Sunup Brings

Zerial spoke. 'Will you talk to me now, Wefi?'
Asha returned home after moonrise without a word, and since then Zerial has not been able to get a word out of her. Now he turns to Asha as they both lay amidst their furs, warding off the cold as best they can. Sunup is just a little away, and Asha is not looking forward to it.

'I do not know how to describe it, Hasban It was... like a nightmare,' she said.
'A nightmare? What do you mean?'
'He's dangerous, Zerial. There is something *dark* inside Apius. I know there is.'
'You have thought so for some time.'
'I know! I am trying to tell you what happened!'
'Of course, I am sorry. Please, Asha, I want to know.'
'He called it First Worship.'
'First Worship? What does that mean?'
'It was a... celebration. I don't know. I can't...'
'Shhh. You don't have to tell me now, or ever, if you don't want to. I will understand.'
'Thank you, Hasban'
'You know that I am here. And I love you.'
'I love you too, Zerial.'
She settles into his arms, trying to forget all about last night. Anything good to help her forget.

***

Across Genem, the sunup reveals an entirely different scene. Over a hundred Noukari begin to rise from what little, fitful sleep they had. Their slumber was the result of whatever distraction they chose - full stomachs, tired limbs, broken bones. The smell from the clearing is a blend of blood, sweat and vomit. Apius has slept in the clearing, wanting to ensure he witnesses the entirety of First Worship. His head is clear as he watches the villagers rise, stumbling to their feet. There are looks of confusion, even despair, and Apius knows he must move quickly to halt those feelings. They should be filled with pride, satisfaction at the pleasure they allowed themselves. First Worship should - *will* - never be the source of shame.

'My brothers and sisters, rise to face the sunup!'

The blurry stares of the wakeful turn his way, while others stir at the opening proclamation.

'I understand what it is you feel. Some of you are afraid. Some of you are not proud of yourselves. Some of you want to forget how you behaved. But you must not feel any of these things! This is a night that we shall all recall forever. First Worship was the first night that we have truly lived! We have let go of duty and responsibility, and celebrated and rejoiced! We have finally made the most of the life that the gods have granted us!'

In moments the crowd is stirred to full alertness, and all the eyes in the clearing are upon the Re'Nuck. 'Come, brothers and sisters. Let us retire to the temple and share our joy with the Animex!'

The cheer that follows is subdued, but Apius is little surprised at that. Their minds have been distracted from the negativity that threatened to swamp them, and he knows that he has already started to turn them around. A swift sermon and they will look gladly upon First Worship.

As Apius leads his followers into the temple, he notices the last of them - the five fighters from last night, each limping and bruised. The aggression that existed between them has now dissipated, and they pass through the door in unity. Remarkable, thinks Apius, that such fury could be forgotten so quickly.

***

Asha heads to the fields after a disturbed night's sleep, still determined to carry out her role. The pathways remain quiet, and she wonders just how many made it back home last night. She shudders to think of what might have gone on in that clearing. What did Apius hope to achieve by encouraging his followers to let out the worst of their nature?

When Asha arrives to the fields, she finds them every bit as quiet as the remainder of Genem. There are nods of greeting, uneasy waves, but no real bonhomie. Asha can see her own worries reflected in her fellows. She smiles to think that at least Zerial stayed waiting for her, but how many lost their Wefi and their Hasban for a night? How many had to lie alone in their furs?

When Asha arrives at her quadrant, she is unsurprised to find that she is the only one there. Still, she picks up her rake and water bucket and gets to work. She still believes this is the most important thing – more so than worship, or self-enjoyment, perhaps more so even than her own wellbeing.

It is as she gets to work that she sees something that finally improves her mood – the first sprouting plant, peering up from beneath the soil.

THE WAY OF THE ANIMEXIAN

Apius looks out from his window across the village of Genem. He feels an immense sense of pride as he watches his people go about their business. He smiles. *His* people. It is incredible, he reflects, the difference a single sunup can make. The triumph of First Worship is behind him, but he knows that is the first of many such victories for Animexianism.

First Worship was a great start. But it was just the beginning – there is much more to be done.

Starting with the book.

He looks over to the pile of papyrus, some filled and some empty. So many sermons, so many fine words, but so much of it is only thought, he now realises. Where is the reality? How can his people apply these teachings to their everyday lives? What will separate his followers from the remaining non-believers?

This is his next dilemma to deal with. First Worship must remain a one-off, but is there some way to recapture that mood, that feeling?

Picking up his quill and opening his ink, Apius redirects his attention to his book.

What is it to be a true Animexian? It means many things, and is far more than a simple belief. In accepting the truth of the Animex as gods, and the doctrine that entails, a person's behaviour – and a person's mind – must change. The Noukari have spent their earlier days within a society that is rigid, unwavering, refusing to bend to new ideas. Stoic in their determination to build a society, there has been no time for thought, no time to reflect on what the gods would ask of them.

At the heart of the religion, of course, is belief. Acknowledging the truth that the Animex created us is not hard – all Genem knows this. But the acceptance that this makes them gods is still resisted by some. These unbelievers must not be frowned upon, but simply spoken to, educated and, in time, converted. The Noukari are not a race given to violence.

Apius pauses here, recalling for a brief moment the brutal combat between the five fighters of last night. He debates crossing out his previous statement, but decides to let it stand. Does one exception change things?

The battle that we must fight with those who refuse to join us is a mental one. With words we can change thoughts, change hearts, and this is how we must proceed. The true Animexian does not settle for their own belief – he tries to instil it in others around them. The mission is now – and will continue to be – to bring every one of the Noukari into our fold.

Belief we have established as the core of our religion, and the desire to pass on that belief. But how does our belief alter our lives? Non-believers have always devoted themselves to duty. They till the fields, build the tenements, create tools. Why should the Noukari as a race be denied the opportunity to explore their pleasures? What time have we had to find out what the foods of the forest taste like, and lose ourselves to the music that we have barely had the chance to play? Whether the sun or the two moons ride high in the sky, we do things because we must, not because we want to.

What kind of god creates a race in order to give them this life? What god wants to see his children subjugate themselves in this manner? Pleasure should be part of the life of the Noukari, every bit as much as those tasks. And the Animexian way of life will be one that allows pleasure. This is the second principle of our religion, the exploration of pleasures. Each may have his own – no two people are alike, and these differences shall grow greater over time as each finds the delights that have so far been hidden to them. It might be the simplest of things – walking through the trees of the forests, swimming in the streams, perhaps even reading these very words. It might be more complicated. Maybe future generations will want to write books of their own, tell the stories of their lives, chronicle the growth of our culture. A full written history of the Noukari may emerge, but only if people desire it to happen. Others may find joy in food, creating new *flavours, meals we have yet to imagine. These things must be encouraged – food must not be another part of our duty, but an avenue of pleasure! And so for music, and the nights where we lie with those closest to us.*

Apius stops, placing the quill down deliberately. He looks back at his hut, and with his written words fresh in his mind it suddenly feels very empty. The furs on the floor are made for only one, the table he sits at has only one chair. His larder contains food to sustain one person. Such things he has never considered before. Why did he refuse to be matched when the initial pairings of Wefi and Hasban were made? What do those titles even mean to those within Genem? He has never had the chance to find out, and certainly has no inclination to ask. But why did the idea never appeal to him? When so many wanted companionship, he sought isolation. All had the option to live alone. Few took that up, but Apius was among them.

Was that the gods of the Animex somehow singling him out? His duty – his only duty – is to the Animex and to his people. And this book remains vital to that duty.

So all Animexians must unite, not only in those duties that they see fit, but in their pursuits of pleasure. A life filled with drudgery and labour is no life fit for the children of gods.

Apius places down the quill, content with his night's work. The book is almost complete, and soon he will be ready to reveal it to all of his congregation.

***

Life has begun to settle back into some kind of routine in Genem. For some life remains unaltered, but for others things have changed inexorably. They head to the temple each sunup, ready to hear the words of the Re'Nuck as handed down by the Animex, and again as the moons begin to rise. They talk much of the gods and their second-hand proclamations.

But none of them speaks of First Worship.

This is not out of shame, or disgust at their actions. No,

they enjoy the secrecy, another element of the pleasure that night brought. They may smile at each other, or exchange meaningful glances, but there is nothing by way of words to communicate those feelings. Perhaps in the future the true meaning of First Worship can be passed on to all. But for now it stays a delicious secret.

Whatever duty they hold, they will always have that. Some of these pleasures are flaunted, while other truly remain unknown to those around them. In selective huts, feasts are held to echo that of First Worship itself, the gathered food wolfed down animalistically. Many people do just a minimum of duties before going on runs through the jungles, unsanctioned hunts, all carried out in the darkness of moonrise. Their lives are like they have never been before, the solidity of duty giving way to the fluidity of pleasure.

The division that was once just in attitude is now something far more.

Asha sees it, of course, or at least some of it. She knows who was in that crowd, and sees the change in them. They gave in to something that night, a part of themselves emerging that had never been seen before. Had it even existed before, she wonders, or did Apius somehow give rise to it with his rhetoric, inducing an otherwise impossible frenzy?

But what happened that night is none of her concern. She has another matter on her mind entirely - a single, precious object she holds tight in her hand. It takes her a few minutes to seek out Ajerus, who is checking on Leranus's work in his quadrant.

'Asha. A surprise to see you.'

'Surprise? Why?'

'Well... after what happened...'

'Look, we can forget about that. I find it hard to understand why you did it, but I know you were trying to act for the best.'

'Thank you, Asha.'

'But there is another reason I'm here.'

'Of course.'

'Out in my quadrant... well, I know we are on the outskirts, but...'

'What happened in your quadrant?'

Asha doesn't answer with words, but opens her hand to show the simple vegetable that sits in her palm. Ajerus's face is filled with shock as he leans down to take a closer look, not even daring to take it out of her hand at first.

'This *grew* in your quadrant?'

'Of course. Where else would it come from?'

'I can hardly believe it. This is wonderful. It feels like a miracle!'

'A miracle? Ajerus, must you get so carried away?'

'Carried away? We have waited so many sunups for this, and finally it is here!'

That does not make it a miracle, Ajerus.

She speaks forcefully into his mind, keeping this conversation between the two of them.

I do not want you to speak to me in this manner, Asha.

What do you mean? Against your religion?

Reaching into my mind.

Why not?

Because it unsettles me. I do not know how it is we can do this, but I dislike it.

How so?

It is only you who is willing to speak to me like this. It is not fitting.

Fitting? You would prefer if your Wefi spoke to you in this manner?

I do not want anyone to speak to me in this manner. We were given tongues for a reason.

Perhaps we were also given this manner of speech for a reason.

Stop, Asha! We must stop speaking like this!

Why, Ajerus? Why is this matter so important to you?

It has... opened some kind of door, Asha. I cannot understand how it has happened, but...

Please, Ajerus. I have to know why.

I hear you, Asha. I... I had thought it would be the same for you.

You hear me? What do you mean, hear me?

There's no logic to it, Asha. But sometimes your thoughts will suddenly infiltrate my mind.

How much have you... how much do you listen to me?

I try to block it out, Asha. I am no voyeur. I have no wish to see into your mind. But... it is beyond my control.

How has this happened?

I do not know, Asha! If only I did know, I would make it cease! I have never heard one of your thoughts. Not unbidden. Not without your permission.

This is precisely what I mean! You play with this way of communication as though it is nothing, but now you realise how little you understand! You have opened your thoughts to me, and now that access is somehow unchecked. I can only hope that by stopping, it will come to an end.

Asha pauses in a moment of decision.

'Very well, Ajerus. I am sorry this has come about.'

'There is no need to apologise. You had no way of knowing this would happen.'

'And neither did you.'

'Let us speak no more of it. I intended to bring you good news, Ajerus!'

His face breaks into a smile, so different from just moments before.

'Yes, indeed. This could signal a new food source, a new hope for a simpler life for all of us!'

'What will we do?'

'I suppose we need to concentrate out efforts on your quadrant, and this plant.'

'What do you call it?'

'The calionus. I've tried a few that have been foraged – quite delicious, in fact.'

'There's not much to it.'

'Still, if we could grow them in a sufficient quantity, they could prove to be quite a food source. Why don't you try it?'

'Try it? Don't we have to keep this?'

'Why would we have to keep it? We know about it, and you've shown it to me. I don't see any reason that we need it as a souvenir. Go ahead, you might enjoy it.'

Asha looks at him suspiciously. *You might enjoy it.*

'And I suppose that's just what you'd like, isn't it, Ajerus?'

'What do you mean?'

'For me to start enjoying myself. For me to give in to my... *urges.*'

'Urges? It's just a vegetable, Asha. Nothing more.'

'There is something more, and you and I both know it. I will not be like *you*. You can keep your pleasures to yourself!'

Her piece said, Asha throws the calionus at him, leaving him trying to catch it before it falls to the soil.

WORDS, THOUGHTS

Zerial returns to his hut to find Asha sat down on the floor. The chair and the furs are both undisturbed, and Zerial knows that his Wefi has been there for some time. She doesn't even look up at him as he comes in - she simply keeps her head down, face towards the floor. 'Asha? Wefi? Is something the matter?'

'Is something the matter? Such a question, Hasban Do you know me so little?'

'What is it, my love?'

'There is much wrong in Genem, Hasban This village has... suffered in recent sunups.'

'Suffered? Much seems the same to me.'

For the first time she looks up to him. Her eyes are rimmed with the red of tears, and they burn into him with fury.

'The same? Nothing is the *same*, Zerial! Do you need see the changes in the streets out there, the people around you?'

'What changes, Wefi?'

'How can you be so blind to what goes on around you? Do you see anything? The sly grins, the secret meetings, the indulgences that happen beneath the surface?'

'Please, calm down, Asha. Tell me. I want to understand.'

'You notice the physical and nothing more. You have not seen the shift within our friends, our acquaintances. Our people are changing at their core!'

'You exaggerate, Wefi. You have spent too much time worrying about this religion, sniffing around Apius and the temple.'

'I did all of that because I want to *stop* him!'

'Stop him. *Stop him!* Who says that he can be stopped? And what makes it your duty to do so?'

'No-one else has made it their duty. I notice you have not made efforts to help me!'

'Asha, you have a strong conscience, a powerful spirit. I knew all of these things when you and I became Wefi and Hasban But I beg you not to pursue this. Apius has many people here in Genem in the palm of his hand, for better or worse. Our people are young, Asha. We are learning. We are changing. In a few sunups this whole thing may have passed us by, and everyone will have forgotten the name of Apius.'

'I don't think that will happen.'

'But you don't *know* that. Let this run its course. Trust your fellows.'

'You don't understand, Zerial. I knew that you could not.'

'And neither do you understand what I am saying. Let us speak no more of it!'

And do what? Sit here in silence until sunup?

Zerial stares at her, slack-jawed. His mouth moves but no words emerge. Asha realises that she has never spoken to her husband without words in this way, the mental projection new to him.

'What are you doing, Asha?'

'I am simply... speaking to you.'

'No you are not. This is speaking, voice to voice. What you did was... something else.'

'And what of it? Are you afraid?'

'Afraid...? Perhaps I am.'

What is there to be scared of? It is just another way of communicating.

Zerial continues to look uncertain, refusing to respond to her mind-words in kind.

'You know there is more to it than that.'

'It is not forbidden, or disallowed.'

'You have done it before, haven't you? You are too relaxed, it comes too easily.'

'What does it matter?'

'What does it matter? It matters because all of a sudden I

found out my Wefi is a woman I hardly know! I never had you down for an activist, but I have tried to live with that. But this... who else have you spoken to in this way?'

'Just Ajerus.'

'From the fields?' Why him? How did it happen?'

'I wish I knew why, or how. We were having a conversation... an argument, really, and then it just happened. Somehow we were talking with minds rather than lips. It could have been anyone...'

'Could it? Is that how it works?'

'What do we know about it, Zerial? I know nothing of how it works, because there is some... unspoken rule that we use our words and nothing else! In all our sunups we could have learned everything about this ability, but people are so afraid! People do not want to act for themselves!'

'You should watch your tongue, Asha.'

'Now *you* order me around as well? Is that what being a Hasban is all about?'

'I order you nothing, Wefi. I know better than to expect you to listen to me. But you go too far with what you say.'

'I only speak the truth, Zerial!'

'And there is another who claims the very same. You risk becoming as bad as him!'

'Do not say that to me.'

'Are you so free to dispense the truth, yet so unwilling to hear it?'

'This conversation is over.'

Asha brushes past her Hasban as she says this, heading towards the doorway of their hut.

I will not be back, Zerial. If this is how you treat me, I will not be back.

***

Asha wanders the streets of Genem, unsure of where to go. She is furious at Zerial, but also rages at herself. She has been too soft for too long, standing by and watching as the cult that Apius has developed has grown and grown. She has been exiled from those she once shared a quadrant in the fields with, fallen out with her Hasban, and found herself wandering with no home. It is then that she hears something that heartens her, makes her smile.

Asha, are you there?
Ajerus?
You can hear me. I wasn't sure if you'd be able to.
Are you nearby?
I don't know, where are you?
Can you reach me anywhere? Is that how it works?
It might be. Perhaps the link gets stronger the more we talk like this.
That makes sense. Asha...
How much did you hear?
Most of it. More than I wanted to, rest assured.
I know, Ajerus. I have no reason to doubt you.
Do you know where my hut is?
Your hut? I think so. But what about your Wefi...
What do you mean?
Would she not...

Asha lets the thought dangle, not quite sure how to complete it.

I invited you to help you, as a friend. I have no doubt Harila will understand.

Thank you, Ajerus.

I don't know what will happen after tonight. I cannot take you in indefinitely.

I know. Tonight will be enough. I will... have to figure something out after that.

I will talk to Harila before you arrive.

Asha wends her way round the pathways of Genem, again amazed at how much the simple village has developed around her. Despite everything, is it a strange pleasure to walk through the streets and know the progress the Noukari have made. She still recalls those first days trying to shelter under trees or in shallow-dug holes, wet and cold from the driving rains. So few sunups and here is a settlement, filled with homes robust enough to withstand Noukaria's weather and inhabited by couples where there were once only individuals. A swell of pride fills her, but is tinged with the sadness of recent developments. She knows as well as anyone that the partnership of Wefi and Hasban is supposed to last until death, but how can she go back? She pushes the thought aside, focusing only on the present. Many things have changed of late – perhaps the unbreakable nature of those bonds can be altered also. Was it ever reasonable to expect every pairing to be compatible?

But she knows she cannot run from those problems forever.

Tonight she will stay with Ajerus, but on the sunup she knows she must face Zerial once more.

The Pages Revealed

Apius has barely slept as a result of his own excitement. He relishes the journey to the temple, taking the longest way round. This way he gets to see most of his followers. He greets each with warm smiles and simple prayers, and promises a special sermon today. There are still those who shy away from him, avoid eye contact, ignore his greetings. He feels a strange sort of frustration with them, not borne of anger but of disbelief. How could anyone on Noukaria still doubt? They will come around in time, he reassures himself. In sunups his faith has grown from a handful of followers to almost half of Genem. The rest will join them in time.

By the time he arrives at the temple, he is pleased to see the rows of seats already half-full and more people arriving by the moment. He smiles to himself, the nervousness of his early days as Re'Nuck now gone. The title is his every bit as much as the very name he was granted.

Once the temple is full, Apius bids the doors to be closed and reaches down to the floor beneath his altar. The silence is expectant, and he allows it to play out for a moment before placing the bound papyrus on the table before him. As always, Viarus is sat in the front row, and he can feel the expectancy in him as their eyes meet.

Yes, this is it.

Apius feels the words slip from his mind rather than being pre-considered, the mind-speech beyond his control. Viarus simply smiles, either refusing or unable to reply into the Re'Nuck's thoughts. They have never communicated this way before, but it does not feel uncomfortable, the link between them is such.

'My brothers, my sisters, I have spoken much for many

sunups about the Animex. At First Worship, we started down a most important road, taking our first steps towards the discovery of what gives us pleasure. Each one of us chose their own path.'

Apius is pleased to see a few nods and subtle grins among the crowd. They remember it well, and the shame that immediately followed it is now eradicated.

'I have been keeping a secret from you, brothers and sisters. But I have only kept this secret because I *had* to do so, until the time was right. You may have wondered where these sermons emerged from. The Animex have delivered their words and wishes to me. And I have not just heard them - I have committed them *to page*. Before me, on this very altar, sits the masterwork of Animexianism. I have worked beneath both sun and moons to create this book, with the help of the gods themselves! No longer will the way of the Animexian be merely spoken, but we will be able to read these words, share them with all Noukari. I give you my gift - The Book of Apius!'

The crowd surges to their feet, applauding furiously, cheering at the top of their voices. The cacophony of sound must surely reach even the ears of the distant gods. Apius lets them have their moment, bowing to his flock before bidding them back to silence. The din takes some time to cease.

'And this sunup I must read to you a most important section of this tome. We have talked much about the gods themselves, but what of us? The Animex have given so much to us freely, and as yet all we have been able to return is our praise. Is there more we can do? Can we make our fathers proud of their children? We have taken belief close to our hearts, but we must also let this belief come through in our actions. And so I give you... The Way of the Animexian.'

Apius opens the book and begins to read.

'What is it to be a true Animexian? It means many things, and is far more than a simple belief...

***

The end of his sermon does not see the end of the day's work for Apius. There are few who drift off after he closes his reading, but many stay behind to talk to the Re'Nuck and to see the book for themselves. He watches over the text, anxiously. But he need not worry. His followers are as reverent with the volume as he is, perhaps more so. They turn pages by the corner only, breathing in every word. A small crowd gathers to see the wisdoms imparted there. Those not reading the book bombard the Re'Nuck with questions about it. How did he find the time to write it? How long has he been working on the volume? Why was it essential that the book be kept a secret? He knows that this is the easiest of all to answer.

'In the days when I began this work, our religion was young, and there was much suspicion surrounding it. If the knowledge of the book were to come out, how would the *non-believers* have acted? There is still danger surrounding Animexianism, as long as there are those who oppose us.'

'But surely now...' Hilius begins.

'Now we are stronger, yes. Our numbers swell, and this book grants us more unity than ever before. But do not doubt there are those who would see our religion fail. We must always remain true to our beliefs, and work to change those who have not accepted Animexianism yet.'

One by one the curious drift off, leaving only Apius and his closest of companions alone.

'It is wonderful to finally see the book, Re'Nuck.'

'It is wonderful to *show* the book, Viarus. The people needed to see it.'

'Of course, Re'Nuck.'

'I would like to thank you, Viarus.'

'Thank *me*? What for?'

'I have not forgotten our conversations before this temple even stood. You granted me the title of Re'Nuck, and for that I owe you much. That day I took the first steps on this journey. But I must also thank you for not spreading gossip about this book.'

'I would never have breathed a word, Re'Nuck.'

'I know. I felt safe in telling you. And I should have you do me another service, Viarus.'

'Anything you wish, Re'Nuck.'

'I should like you to come to my hut after each sermon, beginning next sunup.'

'To what purpose?'

'It is important that I do not let this original out of my sight. But it is also crucial that this provides us a way to spread our gospel even further.'

'Of course.'

'So I should like you to come to me and begin to create a copy of this book. And after that another copy. And another after that, until we have enough to give to each believer!'

'It shall be an honour, Re'Nuck.'

'Then it is all the better you should do it.'

'Do you think this will be the final step in converting all of Genem?'

'I hope so, Viarus. I tire of the doubters.'

'Tire of them, Re'Nuck?'

'I should not say such a thing. But as much as the prayers and welcomes from my followers warm me, the ignorance and cold attitude of the others chills me to the bone.'

'Nothing should make you feel that way, Re'Nuck. It is incredible work you do. It will make their worship - when it comes - all the sweeter to hear.'

'Thank you, Viarus. Somehow you always seem to find just the right words.'

'Yes, Re'Nuck.'

Apius is finally alone in his temple, and collapses wearily into a seat. The sermon and all that followed it have left him drained. His attitude to Animexianism is tireless, but the demands on his attention equally are endless. Perhaps the creation of this book will make his work easier.

Confrontations

Asha bids Ajerus a final thank you, but is pleased to leave. It was generous of Ajerus to forget their argument in the fields in her moment of need. But if she had expected less tension than at her own home she was sorely mistaken – Harila had given her the coldest of welcomes, and continued this throughout the moonlit hours. Ajerus had done his best to smooth relations, but it had not worked. Harila kept returning only to one subject – why Asha was there at all.

For now all she can focus on is repairing things with Zerial, and restoring peace in her home.

'Asha! Asha, I would like to speak to you!'

She turns to the direction of the voice. A man approaches keenly, reaching our to take her by the arm, but Asha pulls away from this stranger.

'Who are you?'

'I'm sorry, I shouldn't have approached you like that. We have not yet had the chance to meet.'

'Well introduce yourself now.'

'Of course. My name is Viarus. I am a... close friend of the Re'Nuck.'

'You mean Apius?'

'I mean the Re'Nuck.'

'Very well. So what are you here to discuss?'

'I am here to talk about your behaviour towards the Re'Nuck.'

'I do not consider anything wrong in my behaviour.'

'You have been very aggressive towards him.'

'I have spoken my mind, nothing more. If your *Re'Nuck* cannot stand any criticism, then perhaps he is not best suited to the role.'

'The Re'Nuck does not deserve criticism, especially from you. He is leading us down a great path.'

'And what makes you think that the gods want to be close to *us*? If they sought to keep us close at hand, why are we down here on Noukaria rather than by their side?'

'I am not going to talk religion with a disbeliever.'

'Ah, so you are also unable to swallow any challenge?'

'You speak of that which you do not understand. The Re'Nuck's wisdom is wasted on you.'

'I have heard plenty of the Re'Nuck's words, and seen what your religion is about. I have seen him bring out the worst in our people. You claim to be growing closer to the gods, but the road you are on leads you only to darkness. That is what I understand, what I know.'

'You know *nothing*. I cannot believe the words you have spoken. Many doubt, many have misgivings, many are cautious. That is natural. Where does this resistance in you come from, Asha?'

'From being the only person strong enough to speak out. No-one will act against you because they are afraid.'

'So you intend to act against us?'

'As I have already done so, yes. I have tried to discourage you and your believers, and have met with the same ignorance and stubbornness you show.'

'That is merely to speak against us. Words can only do so much.'

'We have already seen how much words can do.'

'So you intend to do more?'

'Perhaps. I intend to stop you and the insanity you have dubbed Animexianism. If I can do that with talk, I am happy to leave it there. If it takes more, I am willing to go further.'

'There are many who would oppose you.'

'Perhaps there are more who would support me than you think. You assume superiority, that your religion has power because of a vast temple and a crowd hearing empty words. There are many more people here in Genem. We have always been a society where none seek to rise above their station. Apius has put paid to that.'

'The Re'Nuck has risen through the strength of his belief, his communion with the gods.'

'Just ensure that you - and your Re'Nuck - stay out of my way. I do not give up easily.'

'The Re'Nuck will hear of this. And all his followers shall know to. You have entered something you cannot possibly win.'

'We shall see.'

***

When she arrives at her hut, she sees her Hasban still laid in the furs on the floor. For a moment she takes him as being asleep, but he turns sharply to face her. She can see that he has been crying, a telltale redness around the eyes, and her heart softens.

'You're back,' he says icily.

'I wanted to come back and apologise.'

'And what are you apologising for?'

'Everything. My behaviour, my words.'

'And your thoughts, don't forget those. I know exactly where you were last night. I am no fool.'

'I wandered around for a while...'

'...before you ran to *him*, of course.'

'Ajerus? I did not run to him. I was lost... I did not know what to do.'

'But he was first on your mind. As I am sure you are first on his.'

'What are you implying, Zerial?'

'I shall say it outright. I am your Hasban, and you are supposed to talk to *me*, whatever the difficulty might be. We should seek to solve whatever problems we have amongst ourselves, not by drawing others in. What did you tell him?'

'Very little. His Wefi was not welcoming.'

'Of a second woman in her house? Such a surprise. There are many in Genem who would gladly have taken you in. Even a night underneath the moons would have done you no harm.

But you went to him, because you are in love with him!'

'Ajerus? Surely you jest? He is a damned Animexian!'

'But still, this connection is there. This is why you went to him, and this is why he welcomed you. Why must you tinker with that we have so little knowledge of? By opening your mind to him you have opened yourself in an unfamiliar way.'

'I do not love him, Zerial.' Asha speaks low and with candour.

'Perhaps it is not love. That name would not be fitting to it. You are drawn to him, tied together, the two of you. Despite the differences between you...'

'It is not love!'

'No, I believe it is something much deeper. Last night I made some difficult decisions.'

'Decisions? What are you talking about?'

'I have asked some friends to help build me a new home, far from here. There are men alone among us, even some women who live on their own. Such a thing is not unheard of.'

'You are leaving? Such a thing is not even allowed!'

'It is not disallowed either. Nowhere is it written.'

'You cannot do this, Zerial. We can fix things.'

'I don't share that belief. I should have enough shelter for a few sunups, and by that time a functioning home. I shall not return to you tonight. Nor shall I address you as Wefi again.'

'We must talk about this...'

'We have talked more than enough. You will not listen to sense, and pursue a road far from my own. For that reason, I must go. I used to love you, Asha. That is the worst of it all.'

His final words said, Zerial gets up leaves the hut.

The place now seems more foreboding and terrifying than ever. *Her* hut. Not theirs, not even Zerial's. Just *hers*.

There are duties awaiting her, in the fields. There is work to be done, responsibilities to be fulfilled. Everyone must carry out their role.

But all Asha can do right now is cry. Cry, cry until it feels as though the tears must end, but still they continue.

She has lost everything in her own life. And Genem soon stands to lose everything it has.

She knows that the time has come to act. Not to talk, but to *act*.

Facing Conflict

Apius had heard the news, but not seen fit to give it credit. On the very edge of Genem, a simple new hut was coming together. But it would be a home, soon enough.

He approaches tentatively, uncertain of what kind of welcome to expect, but determined to come and offer promises and reassurance. With a delicate knock, the figure sits up, blinking away the last of sleep.

'Hello? Who is it?'

'Zerial? I have come to pay you a visit at this dark hour. My name is Re'Nuck.'

'Your name is *Apius*.'

Apius chuckles. 'You sound much like your Wefi. Remarkable it has come to this.'

'What do you want so soon after sunup? Do you not have a congregation waiting for you?'

'Of course. But my succour is not only reserved for the masses. Many people have sought me out, and I have seen them individually, to offer what comfort I can.'

'I have not sought you out. And I doubt there is any comfort *you* could offer.'

'I did nothing personally to either you or Asha. We have never even spoken!'

'You have spoken more than enough to Asha. Get out of here, Apius. I tire of words. Words on top of more words. They have brought me nothing but misery.'

'It all depends what lay in the words...'

'You do not hear me. No-one seems to hear me. I have no wish to speak to you. When I wish to speak, it will be with someone without their own interests at heart. Take your gods, and your robes, and your fine *words* and begone.'

'I had hoped...'

Apius is unable to finish the sentence, for in moments a disrobed Zerial is out of his furs and bearing down upon him. Grasping the collar of his robe, Zerial lifts the Re'Nuck from his feet so that the two of them are eye to eye. The intensity in those pupils unsettles the helpless Apius.

'I *will... be... heard*, Re'Nuck. Are you so used to filling the air that you have forgotten how to listen? You will go from my hut. You will go about your life. I will go about mine. And we shall *not* cross paths again.'

Apius can only spit out the simplest of words.

'If... that... is what you wish.'

Rather than releasing the Re'Nuck gently, he throws him bodily to the floor. Apius rises slowly. He wants to say something more but, lacking words, he leaves Zerial to his lonely existence.

As Apius crosses Genem for the temple, he as always dispenses his blessings and his words from the gods. But today they are far more rote than usual, falling back on his more practiced lines. His followers seem pleased to hear them nonetheless, and he is able to force a smile onto his face as he speaks and listens. Does he listen, truly listen? He had always thought so, but his altercation with Zerial has left him doubting himself. His followers are precious to him, and he values them immensely. He knows that all he has achieved would have been impossible without them. But does he value them as individuals, or as a mass?

Apius also realises just how close he had come to being the recipient of violence. Until he had seen the fighters at First Worship, he would never have considered such a thing possible. Perhaps they still meet to fight, like so many keeping their pleasures a delightful secret among them.

As he finally reaches the temple, there is only one thought in his mind – could one of the Noukari actually *kill* another?

***

Apius takes a moment to refocus as he enters the temple, stepping calmly and slowly through his congregation. As he reaches the altar, he pauses a moment before speaking. 'My brothers and sisters...'

He musters just four words before the door swings open with a *clang*, pushing some of the crowd at the back of the temple aside with pure force. Apius hates to see that all the attention in the room, even his own, is fixed to the doorway and the figure standing there. He knows the face all too well.

Asha.

However this version of Asha is unlike any he has seen before. Zerial had appeared on the very edge of something, something dark. Asha has surely succumbed to that darkness. She stands naked, her body covered in mud. This gives her the look of a grey phantom, something dead and dangerous. Apius has only once seen a corpse, that of a Vopal, and the colour reminds him of that deathly tone. In one hand she holds the wooden rake which is the symbol of her work. But it is her eyes that are the most arresting – they stare brazenly around the room, and then directly at Apius, with a baleful gaze belying their blue beauty. With her stance, she dares anyone to approach her.

None do.

'Apius!' she cries, and his followers shrink away. For the first time in his temple, the Re'Nuck feels out of control.

'This ends now, Apius.'

'Ends, sister?'

'Do not call me *sister*. I will have no place among the sisters and brothers in these walls. I will not follow your infected creed.'

'You dare profane in this building!'

'I dare. I will dare to do what I want in your house of lies.'

Asha treads through the central aisle, approaching the altar.

'I will not back down from you, Apius, as you are used to so many doing. I have no intention of bowing before you. You and your... *religion* have taken everything from me!'

'You mean your miserable Hasban? Hardly much of a loss!'

'How dare you speak of Zerial! He is twice the man you are!'

'Ask *them*. Ask my people who is the better man.'

'I do not need their opinion. I have stood by long enough and watched this travesty grow out of hand.'

'What do you intend to do, Asha? Are you going to smash this temple? Tear down its decorations, its walls, with that paltry tool of yours? Even if you could, we would willingly rebuild it!'

This brings a few cautious cheers from the crowd. Asha is not about to acknowledge them.

'I have no intention of harming your temple, Re'Nuck. I have come to harm *you*.'

Apius can feel his own face grow pale, the threat of violence meted this morning about to come to an unlikely conclusion. He can feel his body tense, but does now know if it is in readiness to run or fight back. How *would* he even fight back? The wooden rake may not be much of a weapon, but it is more than he can bring to bear. He tries to stutter a reply of some kind as Asha mounts the steps to the altar itself. One of his braver followers, a man he cannot name, leaps up behind Asha and tries to launch a crude attack of his own. Apius never finds out what his intention was, because she turns quickly and lashes out the rake. The clash sends shivers through the Re'Nuck, and the would-be attacker falls by the wayside, knocked silly by the force and hatred behind the blow.

'Do something, brothers and sisters! Take this despoiler away!' Apius finally wrenches from his throat, but the words bring no action. Asha turns to the timid flock, knowing they will do nothing. Many are still transfixed by the prone form lying on the floor, a livid bruise rising on the face. They have never seen an act of violence before, and Asha finds herself delighted by their fear. With a wolfish smile, she says, 'I suggest you leave now. This is between me and your precious leader.'

Apius dives to the floor, as though the altar can offer him some protection. There are only one way out of the temple, and the front door is blocked by Asha's coiled form – and

Apius can hardly believe the sight of his followers leaving him behind! They are afraid, he tries to tell himself, they have no experience of such things. They must be forgiven. I will forgive them. *If I survive this*, he adds morbidly.

She continues her climb of the stairs to the altar, amused at the sight of the Re'Nuck cowering without the strength of numbers to fall back on.

'It is no use trying to hide, Re'Nuck. You would give yourself more honour in facing me.'

Apius gathers all his courage to stand before the feral, aggressive spirit of the Noukari given flesh. Swathed in mud, ready to explode into violence, Asha makes a sight to chill the strongest of their number.

'Thank you, Re'Nuck. At least now you may die with some dignity. Your death will mean the death of your religion, and all the darkness it brings.'

'Animexianism will survive. Someone will step into my place.'

'From among your loyal followers? Those who fled at the first risk to themselves? They are unwilling to put themselves in the line of danger for their precious gods.'

'You speak of darkness, but you are about to commit the darkest of all acts.'

'Do not moralize with me, Apius. My act is the lesser of two darknesses. I have no doubt of that.'

The conversation comes to an abrupt end. Asha leaps up onto the top of the altar, a sinuous and strangely graceful motion, before striking out with the rake. The wood smashes against the side of Apius's skull, sending him sprawling. His fall seems to be impossibly slow, the floor rising towards him with all the speed of a plant's growth. Then comes the sickening impact, one side of his skull staved in by the rake, the other clashing with the solid floor of the temple. *What a strange way to die*, Apius reflects to himself. *With so much yet undone.*

The crack of head and floor is quickly followed by a sound every bit as potent. From the back of the temple, Viarus re-emerges, just in time to see his friend – his leader – crashing to the floor. The sight fills him with a horror and revulsion the likes of which he has never known. From deep within him – a wellspring that has yet to be tapped – he lets out a scream that rings around the temple.

But it does not only echo within the four walls. The psychic scream brings a fresh agony that sears within Apius's mind. He has never felt such pain, a jolt that fights off the threatening unconsciousness with pure mental force. Apius brings his hands to his ears, but it is no good.

So much pain, Viarus!

His mental response has no effect, and the interior screaming simply continues.

He is not the only one to hear it, and Asha turns in shock to see Viarus and his contorted face. Their eyes meet, the avatar of violence and the avatar of pain linking gazes, and Viarus only redoubles the unexpected cacophony. Asha tries to resist it, but the wall of sound builds within her head, impossible to overcome.

She cannot believe what is happening. She was so close to triumph, so close to victory.

She tries to reply with her own cry of rage, a battlecry that builds from her whole being, but even this is just the buzzing of a fly compared to Viarus's brutal noise assault.

Still she tries to keep her feet, take a step to close in on the downed Re'Nuck.

She lifts her left foot, but it does not touch the floor.

Dizziness consumes her. She flails, unbalanced. Tries to restore equilibrium.

Fails.

It is as though she watches the fall through another's eyes. It is another's body that tumbles over the first of the steps. It is another's body that finds no footing.

It is another's skull and spine that shatter on impact.

So close. So close.

Apius has simply concerned himself with trying to drown out the pain of both his physical and mental wounds, but at long last the mental reverberation of Viarus's scream fades away. With that gone, he realises the true extent of his physical injury. He can see blood beneath him, and his vision swims disorientingly. Through watery eyes, he sees Viarus lean down, mouthing words that Apius cannot seem to understand. Is he alive? He thinks he is. The pain makes him believe this is the case.

Viarus reaches out cool hands, delicately holds the Re'Nuck's face, and gently kisses his forehead.

That is the last thing on that sunup to remain clear to him.

Aftermath, Consequences

Apius awakens in a sweltering bed of furs, pushing aside the stifling material weakly. In moments the bedding is off of him and he finds himself laying in a simple robe, drawing in air as though it were the very essence of life itself.

Flashes of the past come back to him. A confusion of hands, the sensation of being lifted. Sunups and moonrises out of an unfamiliar window. Viarus's face, peaceful and benevolent. Viarus's mental voice, a wave of lightning-quick misery.

He tries to rise, but his head feels as though it is made of stone. The weight of it keeps him laid down, at least for now. He can hear a cry from not far away.

'The Re'Nuck is awake!'

Apius does not recognise the voice, but it is followed by a flurry of activity just beyond his peripheral vision. Then he sees a familiar visage at last – Viarus. Of course.

'Thank the gods you have returned to us, Re'Nuck! We have all prayed for you.'

'Viarus... what happened to me? So much feels... unclear.'

'You were attacked, Re'Nuck.'

'You attacked me! I recall it now! I remember the screams...'

'Re'Nuck, surely you know I am capable of no such act. You were attacked by a bitter woman from Genem. Asha, who spoke against you so strongly.'

Asha. The woman. The blow. The blood...

'Of course, Viarus. Forgive me. I am... groggy.'

'This is only natural, after what has happened. She came to the temple, like some uncivilized wild woman. I was afraid.'

'I was afraid also, old friend. There is no shame in fear.'

'She struck down Lineus as he sought to defend you. We

had never seen the like of it. To think of such violence within the temple!'

'How is Lineus?'

'He is well enough. Naturally he is shaken, but his physical wounds were quick to heal.'

'That at least is good news.'

'And then... and then she went for you. Like a Hiyel on the hunt.'

'It is coming back to me, Viarus. Such hatred...'

'I do not think anyone will forget what happened. I doubt it will ever leave their memory.'

'She struck me, yes?'

'I am afraid to say so. And there was much damage done... I must apologise, Re'Nuck! I was supposed to be your closest follower, your friend! And I fled like the rest of them in the face of her!'

'Do not castigate yourself, Via...'

Apius fights his spinning head for a moment.

'I can come back, Re'Nuck, if you do not feel...'

'I am fine, Viarus. Just light-headed. I would like you to stay.'

'Very well, Re'Nuck.'

'You came back, Viarus. You were the only one to do so.'

'I did not know what I was going to do.'

'You saved my life, Viarus. That is the fact of the matter.'

'I do not know what happened, Re'Nuck. I have repeated all of it in my mind so many times...'

'How long have I been here?'

'I am afraid you have been cared for over the last four sunups.'

'Four sunups? So long?'

'I am afraid so. The woman did you substantial damage. You have been attended to by many of your congregation, and the prayers for your wellbeing have been almost constant.'

'And they are appreciated. How long until I am back on my feet?'

'I do not know, Re'Nuck. We must simply monitor you progress. It will do no favours to rush back to the temple and your duties. We all depend on your strength, so you must allow it to return.'

'You are right, of course, Viarus. But I shall become impatient in time.'

'Think of yourself this time, not everyone else. The temple remains full and our belief remains strong. Sermons are still busy...'

'Sermons? Who has been giving sermons?'

'Well... I have, Re'Nuck. I thought that it would be the best thing to do, in your absence.'

'How dare you assume...'

'I assume nothing, I assure you. I was badgered into it. I lay no claim to your authority or your oratory skills. I have merely been caretaking at a time when people have needed their faith.'

Apius can see the logic, although his emotions still rage against it. Viarus has always had a good heart, always aimed to help him with the whole of his being. Misguided or not, this was an action meant well for both him and his flock.

'I apologise, Viarus. You have... done the right thing. Please continue to take sermon in my absence, and let them know that I shall return to them soon.'

'Of course, Re'Nuck.'

'I begin to tire, Viarus. I must rest.'

'As you wish.'

***

Viarus leaves the hut, looking behind at the suddenly fragile-looking form of the Re'Nuck. He breathes a sigh of relief, thankful he had returned. It has been tough to swallow his fear, ready to aid however he could, perhaps offer his own sacrifice in place of the Re'Nuck. While Viarus feels a pride in his importance to Animexianism, he knows his own significance pales next to that of its figurehead. He would have done it gladly too – he had never considered what death might bring, or even what the pain to bring it might feel like.

When he had entered the temple, and seen Asha preparing

for the killing blow, something had happened. Something he had never foreseen. Something he hoped would never happen again. There was no conscious choice in it, no thought process. The mental scream had simply poured from him...

He shakes his head, trying to free himself of the memory. But he knows it will never truly be gone.

***

On the opposite side of Genem, through streetways filled with half-lies and half-truths, there is another man laid prone within his furs. But he is not there because he is injured, at least physically. Zerial has been laid there for sunups, refusing to move, refusing to go and fulfil his duties. The news had been handed to him coldly, uncaringly as he sought to help build what would eventually be a school. He had arrived for a day like any other to be given the most devastating of news. Asha - so long his Wefi - had been killed in the Temple of the Animex. There was little detail more than that, and for sunups Zerial cared little for the details. The bald fact was more than enough.

His mind had turned the very concept over in his mind hundreds of times as he lay still, all energy and enthusiasm sucked away. Dead. How could anyone in Genem *die*? What had caused it? No-one had ever died. No-one had ever seen a corpse on Noukaria, beyond those of the native animals. What had been done with her body? Had she been buried here in Genem, or cast out into the forest? Now the questions hit him with what felt like a physical impact, anger beginning to swamp his sadness. What had *they* done to her, those religious zealots? She had spoken so often of her hatred for them, offered so much resistance with her words. Had she gone one step further than that? Was she driven on by his rejection of her, or was it more to do with damned Ajerus? He will only get the answers he seeks one way. He pushes aside the enveloping furs and rises to stand on unsteady feet.

He looked down at himself in shame. For days he has not eaten, and barely raised the effort to reach out for the bucket of water. He has not even risen to go to the toilet, such was his misery, and he looks down at the state of his body and the furs with disgust. How has he fallen so far? Just ten, twenty sunups ago he had been a loyal Hasban with a happy Wefi, a man who knew his place within society. Now he was barely an animal, spending days wallowing in his self-pity and abject depression. He wants to break down again, but steels himself. There is much to be done.

The first thing he must secure is information. The word first reached him from Lionis, so he will start there. After that? Who knows. Perhaps there will be more violence, this time at his hands.

Unravelling

As Zerial approaches the half-built school, he becomes aware of a hubbub from his fellow workers. They look at him uncertainly. He approaches with all the calmness he can muster, trying to fight the fury that rises within him. He passes many of his colleagues and goes directly to Lionis, who takes a step back as Zerial makes his approach. It was Lionis who first delivered this news, in hard words.

'Zerial! What a surprise...'
'It must be that, Lionis. I would like to talk to you. Alone.'
'Talk? Alone? I am working, Zerial. I have my duties.'
'Funny that did not come above gossip the last time we spoke.'
'I was not gossiping, Zerial...'

Zerial pushes Lionis against the unfinished wall, holding him in place with balled fists on his shoulders. 'You are going to come and talk to me. Your duties will wait, my friend.'

The rest of the group turn their eyes away, afraid to incur Zerial's wrath.

'Let us go for a private discussion, Lionis.'

***

Zerial drags Lionis into a quiet stand of trees just away from the streets of Genem. He tosses him to the floor, where his old 'friend' sits up warily.

'What are you going to do, Zerial? We are not given to violence.'
'I used to think so. But perhaps I was wrong.'
'What are you talking about?'
'I have nothing to lose, Lionis. I am going to find out what happened to Asha, every ugly detail.'

'I had nothing to do with Asha...'

'You *told* me, and to the bargain you cared nothing for my feelings when you did so!'

'I did not mean to be so cold, Zerial. I am sorry if that was how my manner came across. I simply...'

'Do not try and apologise. I want to know one thing.'

'What is that?'

'I want to know what happened to her.'

'I know only the vaguest rumours picked up around the village. There has been much talk, half of it contradicting the other.'

'Try and discern the truth. Indulge me.'

'There is not much known for sure. We know that Asha died, four sunups ago. She died within the walls of the temple, although there are none who claim to have been there or witnessed it.'

'None? So she just... died on her own!'

'I do not know, Zerial! No-one I have spoken to was there, that is all I can say.'

'How did she die? How!'

'The whisper is it was a bump to the head. That's all anyone has said.'

'You know nothing more than that?'

'Why should I? We talk little. We are busy with our work. I have never even been to the temple!'

'I believe you.'

'Are we done? Is our business finished?'

'For now, yes. But do not think that I have forgotten the delight you took in sharing news of my Wefi's death. Now begone.'

Lionis scrambles to his feet, leaving the stand of trees cautiously, watching Zerial as he goes.

***

Zerial sits still in the clearing, trying to calm himself. The temple. Of course. Where else could it have been? The temple she hated so much. The temple that had driven the wedge between them.

Where did that leave him? Was he really willing to take up the same crusade as his lost Wefi, taking on all his fellow men and their beliefs, let alone the venomous Re'Nuck?

With only the faint sound of distant building, he makes a resolution. He knows that he will - that he *must* - continue what Asha started. She would have done so for him, and he cannot bear the thought of any more blood being shed thanks to the madness of that religion. There had never been a death in Genem before its emergence, and he could not stand another person to feel these emotions.

He would begin his own crusade. But this would be devoted to everything that Asha stood for - duty, responsibility, crafting a great society without worrying what any 'gods' may think of it.

And he would start with a visit to the Temple of the Animex.

***

From the edge of the clearing, Zerial watches the followers file into the temple. He tries to count them, but loses track. This is what he is going to have to fight. He has seen them, heard them enough to know that changing that faith is going to be a deep challenge. What if it proves impossible to eradicate those beliefs? What if the religion goes on regardless of his efforts? Asha had tried, and ultimately paid a fatal cost. If he has to die also to succeed, then he will do so gladly.

So much of the future depends on it.

***

Viarus stands behind the altar, nerves consuming him as always. The concept of standing in place of the Re'Nuck has always sat ill with him. But he has done this for his sake, for the sake of Animexianism. He is no natural speaker, and lacks the charisma of their leader. He shakes as he tries to hold the Book of Apius. His voice is often too quiet, even in the echoing walls of the temple.

'Brothers, sisters, I am pleased to welcome you again to sermon. I know many of you have asked questions about the Re'Nuck's health. Today I am delighted to give you good news. Our leader is once more awake, and I have spoken to him. He has endured much, but he still praises the gods of the Animex. He has given us his blessing to continue sermons in his absence, so we may still pray and give worship until he can return to us. And today there is much to celebrate!'

The cheer that rises is the most uproarious that Viarus has heard during his short time as temporary minister. He nods and smiles, letting them have their moment. All too often of late sermon has been short of passion, filled with waiting and expectancy. The noise takes a few moments to settle down, and Viarus reaches for the Book of Apius, ready for today's reading.

Before he can begin, another voice speaks up from the back of the room.

'I would bid you not to open that book, Viarus.'

The tone gives him pause, and he looks to the doorway to see Zerial staring at him unrelentingly. Viarus tries to keep his eyes level with Asha's Hasban, but finds he cannot maintain the gaze.

'What business is it of yours, Zerial? I am here to share the words of the Re'Nuck. Unless you wish to hear them, I suggest that you leave.'

'I shall leave once I have said my piece. I would like all to consider these words before you hear the ramblings of your precious leader. I have come only to let you know that I have lost something, something that meant a great deal to me. I know little of what happened, but within these four walls my Wefi was lost to me. My Wefi *died* in this place. You may be sitting where her corpse lay. There may have been bloodstains on the very seat on which you listen to your sermon. I shall interrupt you no longer, only to say this. I am going to find out what happened to her. And whoever is responsible for her death will be sure to suffer.'

'We have no wish to hear your threats or your morbid rantings. Be gone from this place.'

'I will, for now. But you can expect to see me again.'

Zerial gives a wry smile before pushing his way out of the temple.

The Gathering

A man shouted. 'Zerial! Zerial!'

It is a voice he does not know, but he can hear the man racing towards him at full speed. He swiftly places the latest log in place and turns to greet the sweaty figure.

'What is it, my friend?'

Zerial's work colleagues try to appear as though they are not watching what is going on. There has been a certain unease around him since the incident with Lionis.

'Zerial, I am Olurus.'

'It is good to meet you, Olurus. You seek something from me?'

'I have just heard of your words inside that damned temple.'

'I spoke only what I felt needed to be said.'

'I wanted to congratulate you for having the bravery to speak up. Somebody had to!'

'Thank you, my friend. But your congratulations are unnecessary. If you had been through what I had, you would have done the same thing. Why have you rushed here so?'

'I have come as a messenger today, for our group. We would like you to come and speak to us.'

'A fine invite, but I cannot simply desert my duties here.'

'You have another duty, Zerial. A much greater duty! Please, we would simply ask a few moments.'

Zerial turns to his colleagues, still uncertain of just why he is accepting this invite. Curiosity, he tells himself, nothing more.

'My fellows, I shall return shortly. I will make up however long I am gone later.'

There are quiet nods, the fear of him still writ across faces. In this case it has been a benefit.

'What is this... group all about, Olurus?'

'I would rather you wait to hear it from everyone.'

'I can easily go back to my duties. It is probably where I should be.'

'Please, Zerial! Very well. We share your beliefs, your hatred of those whom follow Animexianism.'

'And you have only just gathered together, for the first time?'

'No. We have been meeting for many sunups.'

'Really? And what have you done in this time?'

'Done? Well... nothing as dramatic as you have. We discuss many different matters, a little more philosophically than many do. But I doubt my words are doing us justice.'

'I see. Where are you taking me?'

'We meet a little outside of Genem. It remains safe that way.'

'Safe? You speak in riddles, Olurus.'

'Everything will make sense in time. Come, we are almost there.'

***

There refers to a ramshackle hut, built with limited materials and limited expertise. Zerial doubts that it would even keep out the rains, but decides to make no comment. The pride with which Olurus presents it seems at odds with its appearance.

'What do you think, Zerial?'

'Quite a location. Well and truly out of the way.'

'That was the intention. Come inside, everyone is keen to meet you.'

Zerial shrugs, following Olurus inside.

'Great news, one and all! Zerial had decided to join us!'

A smattering of applause breaks out, and Zerial suddenly feels very self-conscious. The group inside consists of six people, including Olurus, a mixture of both men and women. His suspicions are confirmed – while his body is muscled from building, these are wan individuals, far more given to cerebral matters. Olurus bids him to sit on the floor, and he joins a circle there. It is moist beneath him, but he makes no complaint. In the middle of the circle there is a pile of papers, and Zerial's curiosity is piqued.

'Welcome all, and especially to our esteemed guest. Thank you for attending this meeting of the A'Nockians.'

Zerial nods, and the speaker introduces herself and the remainder of the group. The apparent 'leader' is called Ameri, a pretty but waifish woman with white eyes. The remainder give only names and no details. When the conversation returns to Ameri, she says more about herself.

'Zerial, it is a delight to meet you at last. We were all distraught to hear of the death of Asha.'

'Asha? What do you know about it?'

'We have continued to ask questions, but little has come to light. She died within the temple, attempting to act against Apius. Many have spoken of the prelude to her death, but no-one can tell of the moment itself.'

'The prelude? What happened?'

'She went into the temple, and frightened the entirety of the congregation. Many have spoken of her... fearsome manner. They insist she went there intent on *killing* the Re'Nuck.'

'Killing him? I do not know...'

'I do not fall on one side or the other. But I am happy to tell you everything I have heard about the matter. One of the congregation attempted to attack her, to protect Apius. She struck him down.'

'Struck him down? With what?'

'Her rake, apparently, from the fields.'

'She went there armed?'

'That much seems sure. Once she had struck the man down, she bid Apius's followers to leave. They did, to a man.'

'Pathetic.'

'Do not be so quick to judge, Zerial. I have no love for the Animexians, nor do any of us. But bear in mind that *violence* is not natural to us. Have you ever seen the sight of blood, felt the fear of someone threatening to dispense pain upon you?'

'No. But I have felt the urge.'

For the first time Ameri has no ready answer. She blanches, just for a moment, before continuing.

'Then perhaps there is more to this than meets the eye. But that is not the important matter now.'

'As you wish. So no-one saw what happened?'

'Not strictly true. A few people have said that one person went back into the temple.'

'Went back in? Who?' Zerial gets up from the floor, standing over Ameri menacingly.

'Do you threaten me also, Zerial? You are not quite what I expected, I must admit, but you have passion. Fire. Please, be seated. No-one knows who it was that went back in.'

Zerial seats himself again. 'I am sorry, Ameri. I have not given myself the greatest of introductions.'

'Do no apologise. Emotions are running higher than ever before. People are confused, uncertain of what comes next. The fact that the Re'Nuck has not returned to sermons has not helped.'

'He has not returned?'

'He was injured in the effort, apparently. Your Wefi showed her ferocious side in more ways than one. For several sunups he has been in ill health.'

'Ill health? Then surely this is our time to strike?'

'Strike? Zerial, you are too quick to leap to aggression.'

'What other solution do your propose? Hmmm? Do the rest of you not have *voices*?!

Olurus is the one to speak up in return. But he chooses to speak in a manner that Zerial has only heard once before.

We each have a voice, Zerial. But we do not speak in the way you might be used to.

Zerial stares deep into the eyes of Olurus.

'I am not going to have this conversation like this.'

Are you like them, too? Ameri intervenes. *In this place we are truly safe from the eyes – and minds – of the rest of Genem.*

'What do you mean, Ameri?'

We are not just here to reinforce the way of life as we used to have it. Many people have never spoken of this ability, let alone explored how it functions, what it means.

'And what does it mean?'

Will you not speak to us as we speak to you?'
'I will not. Now tell me... what does it mean?'
It gives us a means to communicate with those we wish to. For you to hear me I have taken a conscious choice to allow you into my thoughts. I could have blocked you with a simple act of will. Simultaneously I have allowed the remainder of the people in this room into my channel also.
'Channel?'
It seems a fitting choice of word. Voice would be a misnomer, don't you think? Were anyone else in Genem to try and join our conversation, they could not.
'How can you be so sure?'
This is a closed circle within these walls. You hear me because I let you do so. Everyone else hears me for the very same reason. Equally, should they decide they do not wish to hear me, they could block me out also.
'Why can I not block you out?'
Because you have not practiced. You are inexperienced. It is within you, but until you exercise it that powers remains week.
'I want to block you out.'
You cannot, because my mastery is greater than yours. I can reach into your mind – provided you are close enough by – at any time I like. I do not wish to, but that is the nature of the channel.
'Well, what else have you learned in all your study?'
We have conducted many experiments. The reach of any individual's channel is limited. I could not reach into the heart of Genem from here, which is another element of safety in being here. But if we all gather our mental strengths, we can reach much further.
'What do you mean?'
Much like if four or five people set out to shout one person's name, the sound would reach much further. So it is with your mental channel. The force we can combine between us is remarkable. We also found out something else. Something... disturbing.
'Disturbing?'
I am afraid so. We have tried much, some of which has had... a negative impact. Olurus himself is here despite a great pain that I caused him. The mind channel is not only a force that can be used for communication. There is... another use. I hated to do it, but we have

devoted ourselves to uncovering all the knowledge we can. The channel can also be used as an instrument of pain.

'As a weapon?'

If you prefer the term, then yes. But we are not given to violence, Zerial. We must view what has just happened as an aberration. We have debated long and hard whether to share this knowledge with you today, but we believe that you deserve honesty from us.

'Why would you withhold that knowledge?'

Your... diatribe at the temple a few days ago made your intentions very clear.

'My intentions remains unchanged. And I do not need mind-trickery in order to achieve them.'

I am pleased to hear you say that. But you must not pursue this in the manner you have chosen.

'What do you mean?'

While we are opposed to Apius and his religion, we do not condone physical violence in any way. It will only make the situation worse. Asha's death is a tragedy, the worst we have seen, but we cannot let that lead us down a road of retaliation.

'So what do you propose? A peaceful discussion? They will not change their colours.'

We do not expect this to be a process that will be complete next sunup, or the sunup after that. We must bring them around to our ways.

'And what do you have to back up your case? Have you ever spoken to one of them? Heard what they have to say? Apius has blinded them, and you too must be blind if you do not see it!'

Calm your tone, Zerial. Take a look at the book before you.

Zerial leans forward and picks up the book, as delicately as he can. The cover is marked with the intricately written words, *The Book of Truths*. He opens it and scans a few pages.

'I do not have time to read the whole book. What is this?

It is the work I have undertaken ever since I was able to pick up a quill and commit words to page. The Book of Truths is designed to tell only what we can see, what can be proven. The Book of Apius talks much of things that cannot be seen, so this volume is its counter. It gives the story of our history, our growth, all of our joys and troubles.

'You have been working on this for that long? Do you speak of the Animex?'

Of course we speak of them, but not as gods. What evidence is there of that? They are our creators, but does that make them gods? We have created homes and buildings here in Genem. Does that act make us gods? Creation alone is not evidence of godhood.

'So this is your version of the truth? 'What do you intend to do with it?'

We are going to give it to you.

'What? Why would you do such a thing?'

Zerial, today you have shown more fire, more passion than any of us could. These truths must be spread, but we are not the ones to spread them. Our task has been to gather them together, and keep documenting each new development as it happens. Our last chapter speaks of the death of Asha.

'What is the end of the book?'

I do not know. Only you know what that will be. We would ask you to accept the book, and use it. Use it in your crusade against the Re'Nuck and his blasted religion. He can yet be defeated.

'That is what Asha said.'

I understand just how difficult this must be for you. But we both know that Asha would have bid you to continue in her mission. She would have wanted the Re'Nuck stopped at any cost. She gave her life to that cause. Will you do the same?

The Last Visit

As Viarus peers around the door of the hut, he is heartened by what he sees. The Re'Nuck is sat up again and greedily eating fruit. Hewus, his healer, sits to one side, although Viarus remains doubtful of how much his ministrations here helped. The strength of will of the Re'Nuck was surely enough to see him recover alone.

'Viarus! Please, come in. Hewus, would you give us a moment?'

The healer nods before leaving the hut, knowing better than to question his leader.

'It is good to see you again, Re'Nuck, especially in such fine health.'

'Fine is too strong a word. But rest assured I am on the path to recovery. I shall return to my sermons on the sunup. Do you think my congregation will forgive me a shorter reading than usual?'

'They would forgive you anything, so pleased will they be to see you return.'

'Let us hope so. I grow too restless in this bed and within these walls.'

'There is much of which I must speak, Re'Nuck. I apologise for bringing such impositions, but I have... concerns for your safety. For our safety.'

'Concerns? What concerns?'

'A man came to the temple in the midst of one of my... sermons.' Viarus almost stops short of using the world, knowing how his efforts pale in comparison to the Re'Nuck himself. 'He was the Hasban of the woman Asha.'

Apius has no ready answer, the sight of the fearsome woman still fresh within him.

'Who is he? And what does he want?'

'His name is Zerial. He interrupted, and threatened much.'

'Asha's Hasban. Did he harm anyone?'

'No. He was unarmed, and came only to talk. He said that he would end us, and Animexianism.'

'Did he say more?

'No, Re'Nuck.'

'Then why do you fear so? We cannot *be* ended, Viarus. We are strong, and our numbers swell all the time. Half of Genem is with us, and soon the majority of the folk will support us.'

'But...'

'But nothing, Viarus. This man is a crackpot, just like his blasted Wefi. There is no more to be said.'

'If you are sure...'

'Since you have started, there is a matter of which I must speak. A matter of utmost importance.'

'Of course, Re'Nuck.'

'These pests Asha and Zerial have given me all the proof I need to know that this is the right time for this. A ceremony, the vastest Genem has ever seen. A ceremony to dwarf First Worship.'

Viarus nods, delighted to hear the Re'Nuck sermonising once more. His way with words stirs the faith, and Viarus feel privileged to consider himself among his closest servants.

'This shall be the day when the hearts and minds of Genem shall truly be won! Our words have brought many to our banner, but now we shall take the next step!'

Viarus can barely breathe with the excitement, but Apius pauses for a few seconds.

'And you, Viarus, will play a key part within it.'

***

Zerial sits alone in his hut, which has gradually come to resemble a home. It is still irrefutably a home for one, half-filled. He does not know what will become of his and Asha's belongings from their former house, but there is too much pain buried within them. The furs of their bed will sing with misery, the simple furniture cut through with wasted joy. Everything new for a new life.

And a new meaning to that life?

Zerial turns to the book that sits upon the floor. He accepted the volume, grudgingly, not sure what his intentions were. Could a simple *book* truly be enough to destroy Animexianism? Perhaps there is more power in words than he had ever given credit to. A book had given rise to the way of Animexianism itself. And Viarus had been the one reading from it, not the Re'Nuck himself. Did that say that the power was in the words, not the person speaking them?

He curses, shouting into the near-empty hut, uncaring of being heard. Life had been so simple for him, just like anyone else. A simple worker, a man trying to help his village and love his Wefi. The same responsibilities as everyone else. Now there is so much weight placed upon his shoulders!

Calming himself, he seats himself next to the book, and tentatively opens the first page.

The Animex are a new race, and in writing these words I have no concept of what awaits us. Whether this will be a book of joy or misery, I cannot say. All that I can promise is that this tome will be the most complete record of our peoples' growth. How long have we been here? None can surely say, for we spent many sunups as simple beings, huddling together for warmth and safety. No matter how advanced our species may become, we must never lose sight of our humble beginnings. The very act of writing is a testament in itself to what may be achieved.

What do we know of our origins, of those earliest sunups? Many of us have vague recollections, memories that stir within us a kind of shame. I make no apologies for those initial stages of our development. When we first crawled from the pods, we were little more than beasts. Those pods had held us on our journey, although we to this day have no idea where we have travelled from. The metal shells fell apart upon landing, leaving us to fend for ourselves. I can still remember the taste of grubs and insects and the bark from the trees. They offered enough sustenance to us all, for a time. Was our destination point pre-decided by the Animex? Perhaps they knew there would be just enough to sustain until we could develop a true civilisation. The landing spot was even close to the river, a source of clean, clear water.

What else must we say of those early days? It is common knowledge that the Animex were the ones behind our creation. Yet rarely do we question how this is known. It is a sort of shared memory that we cannot trace. Many seemed to forget the metal shells that had carried us. But I did not. I returned to them. And I saw things no-one else has seen, no-one else could claim to know.

Why did I go back? I do not know. Idle curiosity, or something deeper than that? The shells themselves were shattered and broken, silver components scattered as far as they eye could see. Much had no purpose, the simple elements of a wreck, sharp-edged and shining. Yet there were other things that I found, metal with pictures upon them. They piqued my interest at the time, although of course I could not understand their meaning then.

Only looking back now do I realise their significance. These images tell the story of the birth of Noukari.

Zerial pauses as he reads those words, needing a moment to take in their import. A pictorial history of how the Noukari *came to be*? Such a thing could change the entire view of his race forever! How could anyone dream of keeping such a thing secret?

Zerial closes the book, determined to find Ameri and see this incredible sight for himself.

VERSIONS OF THE TRUTH

iarus stares blankly at the Re'Nuck, scarcely able to believe what he has heard.

'You... want to speak to the gods?'

'I want us *all* to speak to the gods, Viarus.'

'How could we even achieve such a thing? And why do you need me?'

'What I speak of is true communication, not the one-way process of worship.'

'You want not only for us to speak to the gods, but for them to speak to us also?'

'Surely that is the very pinnacle of what we could achieve as Animexians? But our voices will not do enough. To achieve this we must transcend the physical and reach another level entirely.'

'You... you speak of the *scream*?'

'You may wish to call it that, Viarus, based upon your experience. But you must realise there is more to it than that. Your voice emerged as a scream, on that occasion. Just bear in mind what you saw, and what your natural reaction would be.'

'Your followers would have been horrified at the sight!'

'Of course they would. Even those yet to accept our religion may have felt the same. But maybe it was the hand of the gods themselves guiding your actions that day, showing us what we must do! Did you never stop to ask why it was only *you* who returned to help me?'

'I came... out of duty. Out of wanting to maintain our faith.'

'All noble purposes, unquestionably, but surely the rest of the congregation feel the same? No, there was a reason it was you above any other – to demonstrate the power at your disposal!'

'Power! If only I could believe I had the power of which you speak!'

'I have witnessed it first-hand, and do not forget that Asha witnessed it as well. It was your power, and your power only, that saved me.'

'There is no power! That scream was beyond my control. I do not even know how it happened!'

'Viarus, please, calm yourself. I realise that we have much to learn of this mental capacity. But what is evident is that you have a great well of potential power. I do not wish to hear that sound again, as I am sure you do not. But what does not yet shine can be made to gleam. We shall take on this endeavour, and take it on willingly. And you shall be at the very centre of it!'

'I... you know that I have never refused you, Re'Nuck. I have always been most loyal. But I cannot do this thing of which you speak. What if I should fail?'

'Viarus, you fail me now by questioning this. There is no way to know if we shall succeed – but we must believe we can, and make the attempt! We have some time before I shall announce it. Come to my hut as usual. The Book is almost copied in its entirety now, yes?'

'Of course, Re'Nuck.'

'Good, very good. Then we shall shift our efforts to this source of power you have. By the time the ceremony comes around, you shall own it rather than the other way around.'

***

Zerial works his way through Genem, frantic, *needing* to obtain the knowledge that has so long been hidden from his people. He does not know where he is going, or who he is looking for. Where does Olurus live? Where does Ameri live? Lost in racing thoughts, he crashes into a woman, sending her sprawling to the floor. He picks her up, apologising but scarcely stopping. Cursing, he pauses. *You have to think. Where are you going to go? How are you going to find them?*

He decides to do something he thought he never could, but he cannot wait any longer.

He walks past the line of huts at the edge of Genem, finds his way deep into a stand of trees and shouts as loud as he can. But the shout has no sound to accompany it, expect in the mind of one distant individual. He is amazed at how naturally the act comes to him.

Ameri? Can you hear me?

The interior voice seems to echo between his ears in a manner he cannot understand. The answer does not come immediately. He takes a deep breath and focuses. He knows so little of how this works. Picturing Ameri's face, trying to remember the sound of her mind-channel, he tries again.

Ameri? Are you there?

This time there is a reply.

Zerial? Is that you?

The response is a whisper, but within seconds Zerial has zeroed in on the source of the channel.

Not so resistant any more, Zerial?

I must see you, Ameri. It is vital. I wish to know more.

Of course.

How will I get to you?

You do not. Simply stay where you are and I shall find you. If I lose sight of you, I will call for you.

Lose sight of me?

Please do not quibble, Zerial. I will be there soon.

Zerial does not to have to wait for long. There is soon enough a rustling through the trees and Ameri emerges. Despite the speed of her travel, she still looks calm and unflustered.

'It turns out I was not so far away.' she says.

Do you not wish to speak via our channels any more?

'I do not wish to speak at all, here. Come with me to my hut. I know what it is you are looking for.'

Zerial silently follows as they leave the forest's edge.

The hut that Ameri calls her own is a simple affair. He is somehow unsurprised to see one of everything inside it. So much like his own. Since their first meeting he had found it hard to picture her with a Hasban Perhaps people could have said the same of Asha - principled, driven, honest.

'This is... pleasant.' he ventures.

'I have never troubled myself with such things. You do

not have to bother with idle conversation. Please, sit down. I will show you what you have come to see.'

She effortlessly switches her voice from mouth to mind.

We shall speak with our thoughts from now on. Focus on me and all will be well.

Of course, Zerial mind-replies. The echo seems to have gone now, either proximity or practice.

I am pleased that the first part of the book intrigued you so.

It will certainly capture the imagination of Genem.

Good. I keep these images hidden as safely as I can.

Ameri rises from her seat and throws the thick furs that constitute her bed aside. They land silently, revealing what looks like a simple dirt floor. But Ameri starts to feel around in the dark soil, soon uncovering a handle amidst it. Pulling sharply, a wooden lid comes away, revealing a modest chest.

For a long time we A'Nockians shared these images, making sure they were with someone at all times. Guarded, I suppose. But I eventually enlisted some help to build this chest.

Once their existence is known, people may come looking.

I fully expect so. In fact, I expect nothing less.

Not all of them may be friendly.

Ameri puts the chest down heavily.

What do you mean?

You speak of using this Book of Truths as a means to refute the word of the Re'Nuck. Do you believe his followers would not come looking, perhaps even aim to destroy these pictures?

Destroy something? Of such value? No, no. The truth will be known.

The Animexians have developed their own version of the truth.

Everyone will want to see these – non-believers and believers alike!

I simply say do not underestimate their potential to... crush what stands in their way. Asha died at their hands. Some pieces of metal would not be beyond them.

I had never considered such a thing. For so many sunups I have looked forward to the moment that these may be revealed. I had pictured such happiness, such celebration! Now they are more important than ever.

I must see them, Ameri.

Of course. Here is all I have.

She lays out three thin sheets of metal, and they both fall into reverent quiet as Zerial looks over them. Each tableau is seared *into* the metal. The creation and development of the pods themselves is a source of fascination, let alone how they could draw *onto* the substance itself.

The first scene depicts two tall and majestic-looking figures stood over a table of some kind. They look something like the Noukari, but if possible their frames are even more gaunt and thin. One holds a long staff, which runs almost the length of his body, while the second looks into a container of some kind. The image shows liquid within the container, but Zerial cannot ascertain what it is.

The second image is on a much larger scale, and shows a huge room in fine detail. In this room are rows upon rows of cylindrical constructs – the seeding pods – which are being loaded with what look like jars. He squints, seeing that there seems to be something within the jars. The beings holding the jars are things the manner of which he has never seen before – he is not even sure how to describe the stocky-looking, brutish beings. Their muscles and limbs are so thick and veined as to make them seem grotesque. Rather than the smooth skin of the Noukari, or their creators, these beings are covered with a dark fur, giving them a wild appearance.

The third image is even more incredible. The sight of the stars is familiar enough, but what inhabits it is entirely unfamiliar. There is something floating in the stars – a huge construct, starkly metal in the manner of the seeding pods, but shaped with such an infinite beauty that Zerial could weep to look at its image. How could it linger so *in* the stars? Such a creation must carry so much weight as to simply tumble downwards! Drawing his eyes away from the centre of the picture, he can see small vessels in the distance. Are they travelling away from this behemoth, or towards it?

What... what do they mean? I do not think I fully understand.

It has taken much for us to understand them, Zerial. We believe this to be our chronology, and to tell the bare bones of our earliest times, before Genem, before Noukaria!

None can remember such a time!

Does that mean such a time does not exist? Did all time start with our existence? Of course not. We believe that there were more pictures such as these that would tell the entirety of this tale. But these three are the only ones to have survived. I have been back to the site of our landing many times, and each time returned empty-handed.

Please, Ameri. I must know what this means!

This first is the very moment of our creation. The man on the right we take for some kind of leader. The man on the left is working on a liquid that holds they key to our life.

How do you know all this?

We A'Nockians have discussed these pictures over many sunups. What follows it helps establish its meaning. Please, let me continue.

Of course.

This second image – as you may have gathered – shows the seeding pods.

I recognise them.

But the creatures in this image are unknown to us. They have certainly never been seen here on Noukaria, at least not in our experience. Perhaps they are another race out there in the stars.

They are awful.

They are different. Perhaps they would think of us as monstrosities.

Ridiculous.

These images open up the world, the stars. You have to realise that our simple lives here are not all that there is! We already know that the Animex exist, gods or no! Why should it just be them and us? Could there not be others?

I suppose, but...

What you must suppose is that our knowledge is limited. We have spent so long believing we know much, but these images reveal how little we truly understand.

You are correct. Please, tell me of the third.

This one we have debated most of all. It seems to defy any logic. The stars can be seen, obviously. In the background you can even see the moons in our sky.

Zerial looks more closely, seeing the twin orbs at the very periphery of the image.

That is... our own sky!

Indeed. What this... giant... is in the centre of it we cannot begin to comprehend. We have developed different opinions on it. Perhaps it is some kind of rock, somehow floating in space. Perhaps it is a village, a settlement contained within finely-honed walls. It could even be a living being!

On such a scale? Surely not!

What other suggestions do you make, Zerial?

I do not know.

Then do not seek to judge the assumptions of others. You are as baffled as we were on our first sitting. Whatever it is, there is one thing not to be disputed – those are the seeding pods.

Zerial inspects more closely again, and can see the contours of the metallic vessels.

I cannot believe it. Are they travelling towards this... thing... or away?

There is, unfortunately, no way to know that.

This picture is nonsensical. There is no way to glean anything from it!

We have reached the same conclusion. But what we can gather from the images is that the Animex either created – or found – a liquid which enabled us to have life. Then they bid the... servants of theirs to place us into the seeding pods. Maybe it was even the servants who built them.

Those brutes? I hardly think so.

Do not be so quick to judge. They may appear rough-edged, but that does not preclude them from having intelligence. This third shows the seeding pods that birthed us. They are on some kind of journey...

Could this... shape... be Noukaria itself?

We had considered it. But we know the soil here gives us a flat surface. This shape is much different.

There are as many questions as answers.

Perhaps. But even those questions must lead us a step closer to the truth.

More versions of the truth.

Just so, Zerial. Just so.

Speaking to Gods

Zerial wastes no time in his own mission, having seen the incredible images. He debates for a while the best way to approach it. Rather than simply openly coming out in open opposition of the Re'Nuck, he decides a more subtle approach is required. So he watches people arrive at the temple both at sunup and moonrise. He tries his best to remember each face, attach names to those he recognises. He knows there is no chance of them joining his cause, at least not initially. He equally knows their *Wefis* and *Hasbans* are unlikely to stand in defiance of them, so he rules them out also.

Whatever happens, he knows the Animexians will have greater numbers than him. But it is not all about numbers. It is about *truth*.

Once he has this list compiled within his mind, he begins to work out some of those who may support him. A few names are obvious. There are those with strong opinions, some who have already spoken out. Some he knows keep silent, but could be worked upon. Himself and the A'Nockians are not enough strength on their own.

A'Nockians. The word resonates in his mind. Until now he had never considered its meaning. *Those who communicate the truth.*

***

Inside the temple itself, people are sitting keenly, awaiting the word of Viarus. He is delighted that he will be able to hand over this duty. They decided between them to keep the return of the Re'Nuck a secret, so as to add even more weight to the proposition he will make. Of course Apius is confident of his power, but does not expect blind obedience. For the ceremony to work there will have to be faith and belief from all involved.

'Welcome to the temple once again, my brothers and sisters,' Viarus opens. 'It is a pleasure to see you all once again.'

There is a half-hearted cheer from the crowd.

'And I am delighted to say that this sunup is the one on which we welcome back our leader. He has fought death, fought pain, and he has won. He has been recovering, as you all know, but much more than that. He has been working, and planning. Today marks a very important sunup in our religion. The return of the Re'Nuck!'

The words had been written, practiced and rehearsed with the Re'Nuck himself. Both he and Viarus know that today must be perfect to ensure the success of the ceremony. Throughout it all, Viarus has been asking himself – *do I truly believe in this?*

Perhaps today will be telling in that.

At this point the Re'Nuck pushes the door open, tottering in with both dignity and determination. The denizens of the temple erupt into a rapturous round of applause. There are hugs, people kissing each other, some reaching our desperately to touch the Re'Nuck. The Re'Nuck does his best to withstand all the attention, unsteady as he may be, dishing out prayers and platitudes as quickly as his lips will allow. It takes time to work through the throng, but eventually he makes his way to the altar at the front. Viarus watches him approach, shakes his hand warmly and squeezes himself into a seat. He will be listening to this with as much interest as anyone.

'My brothers, my sisters. It is wonderful to be back where I truly belong, spreading the word of the gods to you!'

Vast cheers again. From his seat, Viarus feels as though he could be deafened.

'I have been away for too many sunups. It is a momentous occasion to return. My time away has given me much time to think, to reflect. My faith is strengthened by this time, as yours should be.'

The Re'Nuck pauses, and this time there is silence as he waits to go on. None dare interrupt his introspection.

'I have been close to death. I have stared into the eyes of darkness, and I was *saved*. Many of you may be wondering how this came to be, how such a thing could be possible. I say to you – it is the will of the gods! They would not want their messenger taken away, and so I was spared! This has made me look hard at our religion, at all we have done. We have come a long way – this much cannot be denied. We have built this temple, been through the joy of First Worship together, heard the words of the Animex and given praise. And they *have* heard us, brothers and sisters. But is there not more we could do?'

There is a moment's consternation among the crowd, and Viarus himself can feel the shift in mood. They were ready to cheer themselves hoarse in celebration. But now the Re'Nuck asks for more.

'If I were to die, next sunup or the sunup after, what would I be leaving behind? Is my legacy enough? Do the gods know without doubt of our devotion?'

In their seats, people start to look at each other, as though the Re'Nuck is accusing them directly.

'We have taken many steps in our journey, but it is anything but complete. For the gods have given us a great power that we have neglected, the very power that will enable us to take our next step.'

The disconcert among the crowd grows, a few murmurs swiftly spreading. The Re'Nuck tries to bid silence, but for the first time is not obeyed.

'Hear me out, my brothers and sisters!' The Re'Nuck shouts, drawing the attention of most but not all. 'You all know of precisely what I speak – the mental power that lies within all of us! We have all considered it, questioned it, but ultimately *feared* it. I come today to say to you that we need to end the fear of this gift! Because this power has already demonstrated its great importance.'

The Re'Nuck can hardly be heard above the hubbub of the crowd, and for a moment Viarus fears he has lost the audience. He feels compelled to leap to his feet, to do something, but what can he do?

'Please, I ask you to settle down and consider this! I know of what I speak, because it was this extraordinary power that *saved my life!*'

The proclamation smashes the wall of noise to nothing.

'Many of you have asked how my life was saved. The answer to that question lies in those powers which we hide from so much. Asha's attempt on my life only failed because of the bravery - and the incredible mental capacity - of one among you. My saviour's name was Viarus!'

A round of applause breaks out spontaneously, and just for a moment Viarus finds himself the focus of the eyes on the room. It remains an uncomfortable feeling, especially with what the statement really means. For now it lends him admiration, approbation, but once people think about it more...?

'Yes, it was Viarus who returned and dug deep into his gift to save my life. I owe him an eternal debt, for I would not be stood here without him. For those of you who doubt this gift, know that it has ensured your Re'Nuck could continue to lead you on this journey!'

There are nods of assent, and Viarus is relieved to see them.

'What does this have to do with Animexiansm, you may ask. I say to you, everything! I am now surer than ever that this capacity has come direct from the gods. And why should they want to bestow us with this power? There may be reasons, things that we can achieve that we have yet to explore, things that we have not even dreamed of! But I believe that the key reason we were given a mental voice is that we may communicate with the gods themselves, each and every one of us!'

Gasps of amazement. Viarus watches the Re'Nuck smile, seeming to look right at him. Viarus cannot return the smile.

'The gods have communicated to you through me, as you all know. They have already given us so much, but we have not yet been able to reciprocate apart from with our praise. But can you imagine - gathering our mental voices, shouting to the skies so loudly that the gods themselves may hear us – and *respond*! A conversation with a god!'

The silence is reverent, and the Re'Nuck lets is stretch out.

'This ceremony shall be The Summoning – the greatest, the most significant single day our religion has ever known! There is much to be done. We have spent so long shying away from this gift, but now I ask you to embrace it. Explore it. In five sunups, we shall gather here and cry our love and faith without opening our lips! Our brother Viarus has already shown how much can be done, and we all need to follow his path. I shall be offering another sermon each day, between sunup and moonrise. I should ask you all to come here that we may give voice on that momentous day!

***

After a short reading, the Animexians begin to file out of the temple. The Re'Nuck was expecting that to happen – he read with all his usual gusto, but knew that few of the words would get through. But it was important to give a reading to reassure his congregation, and give them time to digest his words. Sending them away so soon would have been a mistake. Those who leave do so uncertainly, but many remain to talk to either him or Viarus. This is something that the Re'Nuck is used to, but Viarus? Apius realises he has suddenly thrust Viarus into stark focus. He know that his belief is unshakeable, as impenetrable as his own. But is this humble man prepared for all the attention?

Viarus is stunned to find himself surrounded by people, each of them besieging him with questions. Their speech is almost too rapid for him to keep up with, a mingled stream of consciousness. He cannot take in a word of it. For a moment it feels as though he is going to lose himself, but he takes a calming breath and begins to speak. He has seen the Re'Nuck do it many times.

'Please, brothers, sisters, I cannot answer all of your

questions at once. Allow me to speak, then you may ask any questions that remain.'

This brings silence. What was I planning to say, Viarus thinks to himself? The silence drags on uncomfortably until he feels that he must say something.

'Much has been said today, and I am in no manner the orator that our Re'Nuck is. Nor do I have his wisdom or insight. What I have - and what I hold close to my heart - is my belief in him, and my belief that everything he does is guided by the gods. The Animex have chosen him - have no doubt of that, and we are lucky to be in the presence of one so chosen. What the Re'Nuck says of the incident in here is true - the sight of his life in peril brought out the potential within me. I have much to learn about this power, as we all do, but if it gives us the chance to speak with the gods, then we owe it to ourselves to *try*!'

'Do you believe it can be done, Viarus?'

'I believe it can. I have seen first-hand what the power of one can offer. If we have the power of a hundred or more, there is no limit to what we can achieve.'

Support

Zerial is the last to enter the hut. Two sunups have passed since his last visit to the temple, and since that time disturbing rumours have circulated around Genem. The entire village has been abuzz with it. Opinions are torn, even among the Animexians. It surprises Zerial, and gives him hope in equal measure. If there is a chink of doubt, then maybe it can be exploited. It is also this rumour that has sparked this meeting. The urgency that the A'Nockians had lacked has suddenly appeared.

Zerial stands before the original A'Nockians, with many more new additions. Ameri asked him to speak, to bring his passion to the fore. Looking at the crowd before him, he now has his doubts. The crowd barely squeezes into the hut, the well-spaced circle of last time forgotten. Still, he is delighted to see so many of his fellows roused to action by what is going on. Ameri stands up, shakes Zerial's hand and briefly introduces him to everyone present. There are faces he knows, as well as many faces new to him.

'Thank you for coming, everybody.' Zerial begins. 'I am not quite sure where to start. You are all here for the same reason as me - we all believe that this movement of Animexianism needs to be stopped. Their ceremony of First Worship was madness, and what he proposes next is *insanity*!'

Ameri nods, and Zerial takes confidence from her approval.

'You have all heard the gossip, and myself and my colleagues have confirmed this as the truth. Can such a thing succeed? They believe so, but we have reason to believe otherwise. Ameri and Olurus, among others, have experimented with the mind-channel, and do not think it can be done. But there is no telling what such an effort could do.

No-one has ever attempted such a thing. One mind-channel can achieve many things. A collection of channels, all transmitting at the same time? *Anything* could happen.'

A hand is raised at the back of the hut, and Zerial bids the man to speak.

'Surely if it is in our heads it can do no harm?'

'That would appear to be the case, at first. But my fellows have done much experimentation with the powers. It may appear to be internal, but the mind-channels can indeed cause pain. Whether their channels can reach the gods is not the question – the concern is the damage such an effort may cause. It may be something that hurts the very people it attempts to help!'

'But what shall we do?' the same voice speaks again.

'We have had little time to think about it, little time to develop a plan. Apius has caught us cold, but we must not rush into our response.'

'How much time do we have?' another voice enquires.

'The ceremony will be taking place in three sunups.'

'Three sunups? What can we do in this time?'

'Please, calm down. It gives us adequate time if we gather our forces.'

'Forces? You speak as if this is combat!'

Zerial can feel this discussion getting away from him, and looks to Ameri pleadingly. Perhaps the female touch will help settle things down. She stands and begins to speak to everyone gathered.

'Please, people, I appeal to you for calm. The situation is extraordinary, that much is clear. The *Re'Nuck* has captured the hearts and minds of many of our number. So far, only Zerial's Wefi has had the courage to stand against them, and look at what happened to her. Sorry, Zerial.'

He nods, knowing what she says is necessary.

'It has been proven that one person alone cannot stand against the cult of Animexianism. Surely two, three, four of us would meet the same fate! We must rally together if we are to stop this madness! Yes, we are afraid. We have tested the powers of the mind-channels, and we know more than any other. But even with our knowledge we have no way to know the result of this. But it could be catastrophic, and so we must step in. We ask for your support in standing against the Animexians, for you to help us in restoring sanity to Genem! We cannot sit back this time and allow them to carry out their ceremonies and their rituals. No more!'

The huddle gathered gives a ragged round of applause, and Ameri signals back to Zerial.

'Thank you, Ameri. We are all afraid, but we all know that this must be stopped. So we ask those of you willing to return to us the same time next sunup so that we may discuss our plans with you. These are not easy times ahead, but there *is* a resolution to be found in this matter.'

***

Once the gaggle of people has drifted off, Zerial exhales deeply and takes his place in the circle next to Ameri. *That did not go well,* he passes through his channel. Ameri is quick to respond.

We placed you in a difficult situation. We should have given you more support.

If I need support from others, then I am no match for Apius.

It is not about who can work a crowd more easily. The vital factor is the truth, and we have that on our side. You have done well to find so many willing to support us.

So many who may be willing to support us. There is no guarantee that any of them will return.

I believe that many of them will do so, Zerial. Some will be too afraid to act, and will prefer to stand by and see what happens. But those who come back will work with us every step of the way.

I am glad that you think so. It does not yet solve our bigger problem.
Which is?
What we propose they do. Getting them here is only the start.
I have been giving the matter much thought. I believe we should invite our adversary to talk to us.
What? Here?

No, of course not. But there must be a place where the group of us could have a conversation?

Apius is aware of where I live now. It is only a simple place, but it would do for the purpose. But he may not be willing to come and visit.

Why so?

There was... conflict between us. I left him with a threat ringing in his ears.

You were upset. Surely he would understand such a thing.

Still, I cannot help but think that the invitation should be extended on my behalf.

Your behalf?

Our behalf. Sorry.

Do not apologise. It is good to hear you thinking of yourself as a leader. But still, you are right. I shall talk to Olurus.

And what do we do if talking fails? I wonder if the Animexians are too stubborn to listen to reason. I have seen them, heard a little of their sermons. I think they would follow Apius in anything.

Talking must be our first recourse. If we cannot win them over with words, then we will consider other actions.

You dance around the subject too much, Ameri.

What do you mean?

Physical force. Violence. If this cannot be settled with words and reason, what else is left?

I do not know. But the concept of violence is repugnant I will not support it, no matter the justification.

I do not believe it is hard to justify. The course Apius proposes places us all in jeopardy. Violence could in the end be a way to limit the pain and injury caused.

You would suggest this without knowing the end result? We all have our own fears as to what may happen. But if we were to resort to violence, we know pain and misery will follow. Apius's course may yet do no harm at all, or cause minimal damage. You would guarantee it with your proposal.

I have proposed nothing. But I have yet to rule it out.

Then I shall do so for you.

Very well. I will leave you to talk to Olurus. The invite must go soon, for time is short.

Of course.

***

The town of Genem is filled with rumour and speculation. People talk uneasily, perhaps unwilling to reveal which side of the argument they are on. Animexians believe and doubt in almost equal measure. Those outside of the religion do not understand and so are afraid. Little is spoken openly. The chance – and the risk – of talking to the gods is an ever-present undercurrent, moving fast beneath the surface of life. But it is undeniably there. A life that was once so simple, filled with immediate physical concerns, is now entering the unfamiliar world of morality and spirituality. The fear that exists is matched only by curiosity. It is as though the village itself is holding its breath, awaiting either disaster or success.

There are very few within the village with an opinion they feel confident enough to express. Zerial is among them, and continues to sow his seeds of discontent against the Animexians as best he can. The Re'Nuck is also definite in his beliefs. He is doing the right thing, and the gods will reward him and all that accompany him in the upcoming effort.

Meanwhile, the Animexians continue to seek their pleasures whilst those outside of their number devote themselves to duty. This merely serves to further the divide between them. The religious among them feast, whilst those in opposition eat meagre rations. The whoops and hollers of play can be heard throughout the jungles at night.

Never before have their people been so far from unity.

***

Each sunup, Viarus heads to the temple at the heat of the day to try and teach a group of willing Animexians to harness the power of their minds. After the first lesson, he lost several students, who were unhappy with what they had seen. This sunup, things are going only marginally better. As he watches the efforts of his 'disciples', he can hear only the faintest of whispers from their minds. He knows the voices remain weak. Why did the Re'Nuck task him with this teaching? He understands little enough of the mind-voice himself, and he does not know how to pass that on. He screeches at them with his inner voice, and their efforts cease.

'Please, I ask you to stop for a moment. You must not make such an *effort*.'

'What do you mean, brother?' a small voice asks.

'The mind-voice does not come about by you thinking about it. It is important that you relax, look inside yourself, *find* the voice rather than trying to force it.'

'But how do we find it?'

Viarus stops himself from snapping out a curse. He must not let his frustration become evident.

'Let us try another approach. How much do you think about it when you speak? Hmmm? How much thought do you put into moving your lips, your tongue?'

'Well... none.' comes an uncertain voice from the rear.

'Precisely. The effort of communication is not in the physical act, but the concentration goes into the words themselves. It is much the same with the interior voice. We do not think about how we get our mind to make sound. We must focus on what it is we want to convey. Please, try again, but do not worry about your mind. Just think it, and think it clearly.'

Viarus watches the groups reform into pairs and attempt mental communication once again. There has been little success so far, and Viarus can feel the strain. His importance to Animexianism has never been so great. He reaches out with his mind, looking for anyone able to grasp the power within them. There is an improvement, a minor one, as he can picks up a few of their conversations. But none of them seem to have the natural affinity he possesses.

'You have made a modicum of progress. Please continue working on your conversations. Focus on the words and nothing else. You will get there.'

Viarus steps down from the altar, heads down the aisle and leaves the temple. He feels a sudden, desperate need to get some fresh air, to be on his own. He inhales deeply, drawing in much air as he is able, calming his humours before returning.

How goes it, Viarus?

The mental voice that reaches into his mind is unfamiliar, and by reflex he blocks out any further attempt at conversation.

'You would rather speak the old-fashioned way? Very well.'

Viarus turns to face the speaker, a man he has never seen before. But the clarity of the mental voice with which he spoke marks him out as something different. A kindred spirit perhaps?

'Who are you, and what brings you here?'

The Noukari before him takes another step forward, offering a handshake.

'My name is Olurus.'

'Viarus.'

'I know your name, my friend. It is well-known around Genem.'

'How can I help you, brother?'

'You and I have much in common, although we have not yet met. We are both close to people that we consider to be great, seconds-in-command in our selected cause.'

'Animexianism is much more than a cause. It is a way of life.'

'Please, Viarus, I have heard enough of your tiresome book.'

'Have you come here simply to insult me, or do you have another purpose?'

'I apologise for my remark. Sometimes my tongue runs away with me.'

'Very well. Now I would bid you to speak your piece.'

'I come here on behalf of both Zerial and Ameri, the heads of our own cause.'

'Zerial? What has he to do with this?'

'You should know too well. It is your religion that brought about the death of his Wefi.'

Viarus tries to block out the mental image of Asha, blackened by dark warpaint, looming to strike down the Re'Nuck.

'It was her own actions that brought about her her death.'

'We disagree on much. Let me come to the point - I am here as an envoy of the A'Nockians, and I would like to request a meeting.'

'What are you talking about?'

'Shall I make it simpler? The A'Nockians are opposed to the Re'Nuck, and the course he proposes.'

'A counter-movement? Interesting. I had heard rumours of such a thing, but I scarcely believed it.'

'Our numbers have grown of late. Popular opinion is mounting against you.'

'We shall see just what is *popular* when the gods converse with us.'

'Prior to that, I am suggesting another conversation takes place. The Re'Nuck, and yourself should you wish, to meet personally with both Ameri and Zerial.'

'Is this a trick? Some kind of trap?'

'Nothing of the sort. Four people talking. That is all we ask. The chance to hear each other before this thing is done.'

'Hmm. I shall pass it to the Re'Nuck and see what his response is. When do you propose?'

'Next sunup, after your morning sermon here. At Zerial's home.'

'Why not here in the temple?'

'We meet at Zerial's hut, or nowhere.'

'An ultimatum? I shall pass that on also. Now, if you will excuse me, I have teachings to return to.'

'Of course.'

Viarus turns away, sweeping back into the temple. Olurus watches him go, not sure the message will ever reach the Re'Nuck.

The Exchange

Zerial spoke outloud. 'I do not know why you even proposed this. They will not come.'

Ameri is surprised to hear Zerial use his real voice, so used has she become to his mind-channel.

'This has to be our starting point. Conversation can lead to resolution, and that is our aim. The first measure of our success is whether they arrive.'

'They will not.'

Just as Zerial says this, in the doorway appears the thin form of Viarus. He looks even more gaunt than usual, his extra responsibilities laying heavy upon him.

'You should not be so doubtful, Zerial.'

'Viarus. What a surprise it is to see you, in tow with your master.'

'What do you mean by that?'

'He meant nothing, Viarus. Relax. We are here to talk, frankly and openly.' Ameri interjects, delivering a silent mental rebuke to Zerial.

'Before the Re'Nuck enters, he asks for a guarantee that there will be no repeat of this last visit here.'

Zerial nods his acquiesce.

'No threat shall be made. As Ameri says, we are here merely to talk.'

'Very well.'

Viarus seats himself on the floor of the modest hut, and the Re'Nuck sweeps in behind him, wearing the finest of his finery. He has dressed up for the occasion, Zerial notes.

Ameri is the one to open proceedings. 'First of all, I would like to thank you both for coming. I realise your time is precious. However I felt that this conversation would be a good use of our time.'

'Your welcome is much appreciated, Ameri.' The Re'Nuck responds. Zerial simply nods. Diplomacy was never his strong point.

'I would also like to lay down the rule that we are not here to discuss things in anger. It is more than apparent that we both have strong viewpoints on this matter, but that does not mean we need to descend to mudslinging. I should hope us all reasonable enough to avoid such a thing.

'Of course. Zerial, do you also agree?' asks Apius.

'Naturally. Things have changed much since your last visit, Re'Nuck.'

'This much is true.'

Ameri slips into the conversation deftly once more.

'We must speak of this ceremony you propose, the attempt to communicate with the Animex.'

'With the *gods*.' Viarus interrupts.

'Please, let us not dispute that matter now. They are the Animex - a name we can both agree on, yes?'

Viarus looks slighted,, but the Re'Nuck speaks for him.

'You are doubters, non-believers. We may call them the Animex for the duration of this meeting.'

'Thank you, Re'Nuck.' Ameri continues. 'I do no doubt that you mean well, and you are doing what you consider correct. I am not here to question the sincerity of your intentions.'

'I should hope not.'

'But we feel this action is unwise. The mind-channel is of course a tempting tool, and something which could possess great power. We have surely only touched the faintest of what it can do.'

'Which is precisely why we propose The Summoning!'

'It is the same reason that we propose caution, Re'Nuck. There is no doubt that this capacity could be of great benefit to us. But at this stage we know remarkably little of its nature. We do not know just how powerful it might be. As much as it may be a great cause for good, we must also acknowledge that it could cause harm.'

'I do not doubt it.'

'Good. Then we are largely in agreement so far. We would ask you... we would submit... that you consider calling off this ceremony.'

'Call it off? Nothing of the kind shall happen!' Viarus squeals. Apius reaches out a hand to calm him before speaking.

'Viarus is too quick to speak, but I am in agreement. The Summoning will go ahead on schedule. We have already worked hard towards it, and are not willing to turn back from this path.'

'You would not consider even a delay?'

'To what end, sister Ameri?'

'Do not call me *sister*.' For the first time Zerial sees Ameri's cool appearance starting to break. 'I would propose that we study further what the mind-channel is capable of. In Genem we have used it little, and never in the kinds of numbers you propose. Let us develop a better picture of the powers at our disposal. Then, in time, you may or may not wish to perform this ritual. If you insist on going ahead – and be assured I am opposed to it – we should at least know that such a ceremony is *safe*.'

'An interesting argument, Ameri, but still no good reason to put off. This will be the ultimate study, the ultimate experiment. And we shall not fail – we shall reach the Animex.'

'You would continue with so little caution? Then you are a bigger fool than I ever expected. If you are so impatient to speak to your precious *gods,* I wish you every luck.'

We need no luck. The Re'Nuck suddenly switches to his mind-channel, projecting loudly and inviting them all in to hear him.

Trying to impress us with this meagre show of power, Apius? You must be desperate. Ameri's reply is every bit as sharp.

The power does not need to come from me, as long as it exists within our ranks.

At this he turns to Viarus, whose face is red with fury. And his mind is the tool to unleash it.

Viarus vents an apocalyptic mental cry that seems to fill not only the hut but the whole of Genem. Ameri falls to the floor, collapsing in a heap. Her own mental sensitivity has worked against her. Zerial struggles to try and help her, the wall of inner sound making it hard to move. He feels as though he is rowing into a current of noise too strong for him. He begins to fall but catches himself, resting on his knees. The Re'Nuck seems somehow immune to the noise. Viarus's face is twisted into a grotesque mask. He has never seen an expression in one of his fellows – utter hatred. There is only one way to respond to such a thing.

With a hatred of his own.

He digs deep into his own well of misery, conjuring all the memories of Asha he can piece together, both happy times and sad. So much loss, all caused by *them*. Viarus and Apius may as well have their blood on her hands.

The wave builds within him. Rises. Rises.

Breaks.

His own mental cry of abhorrence bursts out into the room. It is a howling gale that smashes the scream of Viarus aside, making it seem little more than a whisper. The Re'Nuck's face falls as the agony pours through him. Viarus wears a rictus of shock, as though the sound has yet to even register with him. He tries to conjure some sort of defence, some barrier, but finds it impossible.

The cry becomes louder. Louder, sharper, higher.

Zerial knows that he has done enough, and reaches into his mind-channel to end the shout.

But he cannot.

He had wanted to release all of the emotions he had bottled within him, and they will be released. With or without his permission.

Stop. *Stop!* The inner command does nothing.

It is then that he realises it. He is *enjoying* it.

They hurt him. And now he has the opportunity to hurt them, he is going to take it.

It is as the scream reaches its crescendo, its brutal climax, that Zerial can finally stop hearing the sound of his own fury.

The silence of unconsciousness is all too tempting.

***

Before he is again able to see, he hears the soothing mind-channel of Ameri reaching out to him.
Rest, Zerial. Be at peace.
What happened?
It does not matter now. It is important that you are at peace. You have been through much. It is time for you to be healed.
I do not need any healing.
Just rest. Be healed. Understand that things will all be well. They will be well...
The voice leaves his mind, and blackness returns once more.

***

Zerial becomes dimly aware of his body once again, dimly aware of cold air surrounding him. Before he can open his eyes, or move, the gentle tone reaches him.
There is no need to rise yet, Zerial.
I do not want to sleep any more.
Sleep will help you, restore you.
Restore me?
Shhh, Zerial. You may rest for as many sunups as you please. Sleep, and all will be well.
The siren call is too strong for Zerial to resist.

***

When he next awakens, it is to a jagged reality. The light hurts his eyes, and the hairs on the fur beneath him seem to cut at his sweat-drenched flesh. He pulls the furs away as quickly as he can, surprised to find himself naked. He is even more surprised to see Ameri stood in the doorway, his own doorway, looking calmly in at him. He swiftly recovers the furs to hide his modesty.

'What is going on? What happened?' he asks hurriedly.

'You do not remember?'

'No.'

'Good. It is better you do not. Such an event should be forgotten.'

'So you expect me to simply ignore this blank in my memory?'

'It would serve you well.'

'I intend no such thing!'

Be calm, Zerial. There is no need to become so enraged.

When you seek to disguise the truth from me? When you sssseeek to keep sssssecrets from me?

Zerial, it is important that you rest. Please. I will explain everything in time. But you must rest.

I will ressssst no more! Tell me!

That proclamation is followed by a blunt wall of sound that emerges unbidden from Zerial's mind-channel. Ameri feels it reach out to her, attempts to put out some defence, but is powerless before the mental strike. It feels as though she is being struck with equal force in all parts of her body, a physical impossibility made cerebral reality. She falls before the wave of malice, lying in a wounded heap. The sight snaps Zerial out of his rage, and he runs over to Ameri, who is moaning gently as she tries to clamber back to her feet.

'Ameri! I am so sorry, Ameri. I do not know...'

'I do not know either, Zerial.'

'What do you mean?'

'You truly remember nothing of what happened?'

'Nothing, Ameri. I remember the start of our meeting, the conversation, then... blackness. Please, let me help you to your feet.'

She hesitates, for a moment unwilling to put her hand out, but eventually she concedes and allows him to help her up. As soon as she is steady, she takes a step away from Zerial.

'Something is happening to you, Zerial, and I do not know what. I must discuss it with the others.'

'Please tell me, Ameri. It will not happen again, I assure you.'

'You cannot make such a promise.'

'I can, and do! I swear it upon all I hold dear. All I once held dear.'

'Please, Zerial. Sit, and I shall tell you everything I know.'

Dubiously, he seats himself on the floor. Ameri remains standing.

'You know that we have experimented with the powers that have been granted to us, the mind-channels. We believed that we understood them well, grasped their nature and their limitations.'

'Of course. You told me much of the work you have done.'

'I wonder if all of our efforts were wasted. The meeting... did not go well. We could not get the Re'Nuck to agree to even delay his blasted ceremony. He still intends to go ahead.'

'We must stop him!'

'Please, I must insist that you remain calm. Let me speak, and then I would ask you to speak. I knew that Viarus had been trying to teach people to employ their own, but I could never have guessed at the sort of power he possessed. He... used his channel. It is unlike anything that I have encountered before. He reached out to us and simply - screamed. But it was much more than a sound. It felt to me like a hand reaching into my very mind and twisting, pulling, scratching. I thought there could be no worse agony. He relished it, revelled in the pain he caused. There is something about Viarus that sets him apart from you and I, but I cannot figure out what it might be.'

'He hurt you deeply?'

'I still shudder at the thought of it. Viarus and Apius had me defeated, and I knew you were struggling against the onslaught also. Unlike me, you were able to respond. You... screamed back at him. Right back at him. I have no doubt that you aimed it at them, or at least you intended to do so.'

'I did not know... do I possess so much power?'

'Evidently so. Your scream was different, though no less harrowing. I felt as though Viarus was delivering his attack on purpose. There was premeditation within him.'

'I knew that we should never have trusted them.'

'Do not be side-tracked, Zerial. The true problem lies with *you*.

Viarus may have used his channel for ill, but he was in control of it. Your scream was ragged, unrelenting. You were not in control.'

'I would never...'

'You did not *mean* to hurt me, nor did you want to inflict so much damage upon the Re'Nuck and his compatriot. What is worrying is the result. It implies that there is still much that we have to learn about these powers we have.'

'What do you... think it means?'

'I cannot know, with any certainty. I only have my speculations.'

'Which are what?'

'So far, we have only ever considered the channels to have one element. In our tests, we were always able to control them easily. But there was never any extreme of emotion involved, simply intellectual curiosity. That meeting... was the first time I have ever seen such emotion being expressed. We Noukari are creatures of duty, of responsibility. There have never been such furious emotions raging within us. But I fear it is more complicated than that. We have assumed that all we have is the thoughts that occupy us in the moment. But what if there is another level to the mind? We think on one level of what is immediately in front of us. On a second level, deeper down, there is more going on, things that we do not – or perhaps cannot – acknowledge. It was this second level that overtook you, I think. The surface part of your mind wanted to stop, but the feelings that lay beneath took over.'

'Beneath?'

'Come, Zerial. You and I both know that Asha died within that temple. That does not inspire any fury within you?'

'I have tried to forgive them.'

'But you cannot. I am not judging you, Zerial. What you feel is natural, I am sure any of us would feel the same. Yet you must understand that these feelings make you a liability.'

'What do you mean?'

Ameri sighs, turning away from Zerial for a moment.

'In you, we saw the potential for a leader. We believed in you. But now we know the fire burns too bright within you. We cannot have you involved with the A'Nockians any more. There is too much potential for people to be hurt.'

'I would not...'

'Zerial, please. This is not an easy thing to do. But we must approach this peacefully..'

'So you wish me to step back?'

'I would like that to be the case.'

'I do not think it should be.'

'Zerial, please...'

'Do not plead with me, Ameri. You invited me into this, asked me to support you, and now you will turn your back on me?'

Ameri turns to leave, saying, 'We have to try and achieve this the right way. Just because Viarus delved into his rage does not make it right to respond in kind.'

It is exactly the right way to respond! Do you not see that?

Ameri can only respond in just as firm a manner.

We have lived all of our sunups in peace and cooperation. Once we descend into aggression it can only escalate. We must avoid that path entirely!

You assume that violence must inevitably lead to violence? Surely there must be a victor?

You would call stopping this by force a victory? It is no victory at all if it takes the shape of what you did. It brings only pain and misery.

You are weak, Ameri.

I am stronger than you think. And I have many to support me.

As this thought comes across her channel, Zerial can see many shapes appear in the doorway, the tall forms of ten, twenty Noukari.

What is the meaning of this, Ameri? An ambush?

It is nothing of the sort. We have spoken, and I have given you the chance to see the error of your ways. I have endured much hurt at your hands. If you cannot see that you go too far, we shall simply have to keep you here.

Keep me here! I do not intend to let you do any sssssuch thing!

Zerial can feel the scream building within him, a high-pitched whine. Ameri can feel it building too, and nods to those around her to make their move.

They move too late.

The sound that blasts from Zerial is projected into the

mind of all of those in the hut, an aural knife that cuts the multitude of thoughts. It is only Ameri that is able to stand tall, prepared for the malice that inhabits Zerial. The two of them stare, eye to eye, saying nothing but conveying much. She maintains her mental barrier against him, pushing back the wave of fury, which breaks against the wall she creates.

Stop this, Zerial! What do you think you can achieve?
I can stop them! I will destroy all of you if I have to!
This is not you, Zerial! You have to fight it!
I will fight all of you!

Ameri can feel her resistance breaking, and looks around to her fellows. There is no help forthcoming. Many of them will never have exercised their own mind-channel, let alone encountered anything like this. It is all up to her. She continues to force back the internal howl, the wall within her threatening to crumble under the onslaught.

Zerial, you must not do this!
You cannot stop me!

The force that Zerial projects wavers, just for a moment, and Ameri sees her opportunity. She pushes the wall she has built outwards. She can almost picture the barrier as it crashes into Zerial, who is so concerned with his own assault he can offer no defence. He lets out a cry of anguish, falling to the floor in an abject heap. Ameri crumples just moments after, her energies spent. Some of her colleagues stir with the silence around them, and Ameri finds herself pulled to her feet.

'What was that, Ameri?' Calorus asks.

She takes a deep breath before speaking, her voice broken.

'His mind-channel, his powers of telepathy.'

'How can he do such a thing?'

'We all have it within us, if we choose to acknowledge it. But his powers have become... twisted. This is supposed to be a force for good, something to help our people along.'

'I do not like it, Ameri. I have never felt anything like it.'

'Neither had I. But we must try and remember that Zerial has been through much, endured much of late. It has... done something to him.'

'What shall we do with him?'

'I do not know. We can restrain him physically, but how do you restrain the mind?'

'There may be a way.' pipes up Olurus. There is a plant that grows out in the forests, a rare one. It can put people to sleep.'

'Is it harmful?'

'It cannot be as harmful as leaving him awake.'

'I do not like this, Olurus. We should not be in this situation! You have misjudged him so badly.'

'I thought that...'

'You thought? And you got it wrong. You said we could trust Zerial, that he would be a good leader!'

'He had all of the assets that we were looking for. We already had enough thinkers between us, enough intelligence to understand the problem. We needed somebody who could act.'

'But look at how he has acted! He has hurt all of us, and driven a wedge between us and the Animexians!'

'How was I to know that this lay within him? When he first met us, he knew nothing of the mind-channels, let alone how to use them.'

'He is not using them, Olurus, the channel is using him! I have never seen anyone act in the manner he has. Even Viarus's bitterness was nothing compared to what Zerial has done. Lashing out at the Animexians I can understand, but I cannot forgive lashing out at us.'

'Very well. I will fix it – I will get hold of some sleeproot.'

Ameri's answer comes as a sigh. 'How long will it take?'

'I will attend to it immediately.'

'I expect you back before moonrise. You two, fetch some rope and tie him down. Ensure that he cannot move, whatever he tries to do.'

The two Noukari she addresses nod dumbly, dashing from the hut. Olurus trails out behind them, a man on his own mission. Ameri looks back around the hut to the rest of her supporters, wondering why she even summoned them. It was her own powers that rescued the situation. Whatever physical strength the men possessed, they could not match the power of her mind.

'What are you all standing around for? What are you waiting for?'

None of them respond, and Ameri bites back a curse. Sighing, she dishes out instructions.

'I want five of you to stay in order to hold him down. If he awakens before we can tie him down, I will need you to apply enough force to keep him restrained. The rest of you, just leave, go about your usual business. Rest assured you have been no help at all.'

Chastened, the remainder of the group leaves. She watches those left hold Zerial down, still wondering how it came to this.

The Summoning

Sunup breaks over the horizon, and the time for The Summoning has come.

Viarus awakens with a sick feeling in his stomach, looking out from the window of his hut to see the forests of Noukaria staring back impassively. They care little for the machinations of his race, but simply stand sentinel, looking on with cold indifference. But he knows that something of vast significance is about to happen. Something that could reshape the entire world view of the Noukari. Something that could bring them in contact with the Animex themselves.

Not far away, the Re'Nuck awakens with a feeling of peace. His confidence in the venture remains unshaken, despite the pain he and Viarus have endured to get there. The blast of agony that Zerial brought will stay with him forever, just as the physical pain that Asha caused him. To think one *Hasban* and *Wefi* could cause so much trouble! But their attempts to derail his religion and shake his faith have failed. In fact, they have strengthened his conviction further. Struggle and battle are what make triumph all the sweeter.

Ameri wakens with a dull sense of resignation. For many sunups she has voiced her opposition to the Re'Nuck and his ways, talking to close confidantes of the same mind. Now she cannot help but wonder if she should have done more, made some serious move earlier. Their talk and the experiments have ultimately been for nothing. Even the future of the Book of Truths is uncertain until Zerial comes back to himself. None have been able to find it within his hut, and there is no way to ask him. The temptation of violence and pain was too much for him, and Ameri was the one who had to stand in his path. To be opposing one of her own rather than their true adversaries! It will happen today, she knows. And all she can do is watch and hope.

(MAKE MORE OF THE LOSS OF THE BOOK OF TRUTHS)

And on the very outskirts of Genem, in a small hut for one, a body lies prone and a mind lies quieted within it. Zerial can scarcely feel the rope that ties him down. Every sense is dulled. He barely has any control of his body. The sleeproot is doing its job well, Olurus reflects as he watches him. It is not a task he welcomes, fearing what may happen if he comes back to consciousness. But he has plenty of sleeproot ready. He does not know the true effect of it, but there are more immediate concerns than that. The safety of the A'Nockians, of all Noukari may be at stake.

Genem awaits the proclamations of the gods.

***

Unable to sleep, Viarus decides to head to the temple early. Perhaps there will be some sort of guidance waiting for him there. He looks up at the sky, the sun high above him, and wonders how much further beyond that the Animex lay. If he shouted to the sky with his real voice, how far would that reach? How much louder must his mental shout be to reach whatever place the Animex inhabit? Not for the first time, his doubts rise to the surface. It is then that a clear voice breaks his reverie.

'Wondering just how far it may be?' Apius asks. Viarus turns to face the Re'Nuck, who is in the finest of his ceremonial robes. The occasion calls for nothing less.

'Are you reading my mind, Re'Nuck?'

'No, but I am aware of the doubts you have about The Summoning. I have been from the very start.'

'I can only apologise, Re'Nuck. The magnitude of this...'

'The scale of it is what makes the day so exciting, brother. I respect the fact that you are here in spite of your doubts. Do you know what that shows to me?'

'What?'

'Faith. An almost unlimited supply of it. You have been with me from the very start. You were the first to bestow the title of Re'Nuck upon me. And this next I ask of you is the greatest yet. But you must bear in mind the reason I have asked you is because I have faith. Faith in *you*.'

'Thank you, Re'Nuck. Your words mean much to me.'

'It is a momentous sunup. This is one that we shall never forget. It is when all of the non-believers come to join our faith.'

'It will be wonderful, Re'Nuck. No more arguments. No more doubt.'

'That is the vision, what we always dreamed of. Come, let us spend some time in the temple. It will be the perfect way to begin.'

***

After a stirring sermon, The Summoning is ready to begin. Viarus knows his place – he walks immediately to the centre of the clearing. The power he has is the most potent, and as such he will be the focal point of communication. The clearing soon fills with his fellow believers, with the Re'Nuck presently standing just outside of the circle. Once the shape is complete, and the body of believers is in formation, the Re'Nuck makes his way through the crowd to stand next to Viarus. He grasps Viarus by the shoulder and whispers 'Be strong, my brother.'

Viarus does not even nod in response, and Apius turns to address the gathering. 'My brothers, my sisters, this is a moment we have waited a long time for. The gods have created us, given us life, and watched over us. Now is the time for us to reach out to them, to give them our praise and devotion, and to hear their voices in response. Each of you will know the gods better than ever before!'

There is no cheer within the clearing. The moment is too sombre, too sacrosanct. The Re'Nuck is glad – everyone here is focussed on their task.

'Myself and Viarus shall be at the very heart of the circle, shouting to the Animex with all of our might. But the power of two alone will not suffice. It will require the effort of every one if The Summoning is to succeed! Even if you feel your voice is little more than a whisper, when added to those around you it may be clearly heard. Give everything you have, and we shall bask in glory!'

The Re'Nuck nods to Viarus, knowing that in this situation he commands every bit of respect that he does. He has been the one to teach and train the Animexians to employ their minds.

'Remember everything that we have learned together. The mind is not a muscle, like the tongue or the lips. Forcing things will get you nowhere – the key to what we are about to do is relaxation, a clear mind. I would ask you all to focus only on the words we have rehearsed. It is a simple message, but today it goes on an incredible journey. The words we must all concentrate on are these. *Today we reach out to you, the Animex. We are your loyal and faithful servants.* We must all reach out with these same words so that we may be heard. Is everybody ready?'

There is no response, but Viarus takes it from the mood around him that the collective is prepared. Nodding, he reaches out with his mind. *Then let us begin.*

Viarus is surprised to find the Re'Nuck grasping his hand, a display of solidarity between the two of them. As they link fingers, Viarus begins to pick up the first whispers of the agreed phrase. It is quiet at first, a susurrus that grows out of the silence. There is no noise in the clearing – the wind and the wildlife themselves seem to have been quieted in this moment. The hushed sound that begins to blossom from the gathered minds is messy and garbled, and Viarus a gentle guiding hand.

Listen to those around you. Let us make this sound in unison rather than a broken chorus.

His words seem to have some effect, although it takes time for the inner voices to align. Then the rhythm and pace asserts itself, becoming a hypnotic mantra. With that established, what was ten or twenty voices are now joined by many more. Viarus feels as though he can pick each voice out.

Today we reach out to you, the Animex. We are your loyal and faithful servants.

The sound of the statement grows, a choir now intoning their chant not just at the same pace but also the same tone.

Today we reach out to you, the Animex. We are your loyal and faithful servants.

Viarus is delighted at the sound, an entire religion working together in harmony. What a beautiful occasion! He can feel the Re'Nuck squeeze his hand, but he knows that it is not time for him to step in as yet. Not even half of the voices have tuned in. But with each passing moment, what was a congregation of whispers grows into a loud and clear proclamation. The volume rises, rises, until Viarus feels the time has come. With his own intense power, he knows that he can draw the remainder of the circle into the message. Taking a deep breath, letting the words take over him, he accompanies the rest, a dominating persona among them.

Today we reach out to you, the Animex. We are your loyal and faithful servants!

His own effort lends confidence to those who have kept their mental voices low, attracts the few yet to communicate their part in the message. The sounds builds into a cacophony. The Re'Nuck now takes his place, the voice seeming to echo that of Viarus's own. The build is about to reach a crescendo. The sound has grown and grown, but this must reach beyond the sky to the gods! Unleashing every bit of his potential, Viarus lets loose with a mighty cry.

Today we reach out to you, the Animex! We are your loyal and faithful servants!

The immensity of his voice silences all of those around him. The gathered power seems to disseminate in an instant, replaced with something else entirely.

The interior wails of agony.

It seems at first to be only one individual, a dissenting voice amidst the mental quiet. But then this becomes a mantra of its own, a piercing scream passing from one to another. Viarus can see the followers falling to the floor around him. Their mental screams have stretched into the physical. The wall of misery extends to all levels, a nightmare palimpsest. The Re'Nuck looks around in horror. He digs his nails into Viarus's skin. But there is no response.

Stop this, Viarus! We cannot succeed!

But the plea is lost on Viarus. Despite the pain he can feel, despite the fact he is on his own in the attempt, he calls out to the gods one more time, every pore within his body projecting the message.

TODAY WE REACH OUT TO YOU, THE ANIMEX! WE ARE YOUR LOYAL AND FAITHFUL SERVANTS!

If Viarus could focus on anything but his mind, he would see a wave of force pouring from him. The hell of noise intensifies, the screams doubling, trebling. The message is heard across Genem, too loud to ignore. Viarus manages to blast the words one more time before his energy is drained.

Falling to the floor, Viarus's thoughts are only with the gods.

He does not care what else he has done.

***

The Re'Nuck looks around at the devastation. The toll this effort has taken... tens, maybe a hundred of his followers are insensible, writhing and emitting soft whimpers. Those who stand do so with difficulty, leaning on each other for support. There is an undercurrent of copper and sweat. Apius notices a few people with blood pouring from ears and noses. Who knows what damage is done?

***

Ameri watches from her window, looking out over the clearing. She has seen the people gathered, and for a long time the outwards appearance was that nothing was happening. But of course she knows better. The impression is confirmed as the sound reaches her mind-channel, at first one, then ten, soon too many to count. They hope this mild noise will reach the gods?

It is then that the voice of Viarus arises, and she finds herself filled with fear.

At first the volume is bearable, but greatly increased. The power Viarus possesses is beyond question – she has seen it first hand. But the energy he musters next is beyond conception. The sounds seems to drown out the whole world, flooding not just her mind but all of her senses. She falls weakly to the floor, having no response to such an influx of power. She grits her teeth, determined not to scream, trying to place up her mental wall once again. But each time she tries it is simply swatted aside, unable to withstand the impact. All she can do is try and endure, survive.

That will have to be enough for now.

***

Far from the clearing, there is a solitary hut on the outskirts of town inhabited by two figures. One stands, looking around uneasily, the other is laid on the floor, hands and feet tied with rope. Zerial could not move even if he wished to, so drugged is he. Olurus is there to watch over him but he wanders around uneasily. There is too much else going on for him to concentrate. He wishes he could be closer to the heart of things, able to do something, anything. But the feeling of powerlessness within him has simply grown and grown.

As he paces, he detects a modicum of sound. He can hear the timbre of many individual voices. It is only their distance that makes them appear a murmur, he knows.

Through the mental muttering, a sound comes like the rapid slice of a knife. Olurus grabs at his head, his ears, as the words reach into his him.

TODAY WE REACH OUT TO YOU, THE ANIMEX! WE ARE YOUR LOYAL AND FAITHFUL SERVANTS!

He does his best to drown out the torturing message. But

it is irresistible, its speaker drawing from a well of immense power. As he tumbles to the floor, he can see the walls of the half-built hut buckling, stretching, the wood threatening to break under the strain.

Do we have this power within us? is the last thought he has before unconsciousness claims him.

***

Zerial has nowhere to fall, nowhere to run. So affected is he by the sleeproot that he cannot event lift an arm or a hand to try and block the aural blast.

But he hears the noise. He hears it more sharply than any other.

The sounds comes to him as if through a haze of fog, its location unclear but the cutting power it has all too clear. The dreams that inhabit Zerial's mind are suddenly marked with misery, the images coming too rapidly for him to comprehend, too horrifying for him to interpret...

The corpse of Asha stands before him, her once-beautiful form already marked by decay. Her pale skin is turning to rotted black across her face and arms. She reaches a withered hand out to him, "Zerial, Zerial!" she exclaims. He tries to reply, but somehow finds his lips unable to move, his body unresponsive. Deadened Asha steps forward, placing her lips firmly upon his, the bitter flavour of the afterlife upon her tongue. A handful of maggots eagerly crawl from her throat into his...

Now he is laid, laid very still, willing his arms and legs to move. The limbs disobey him, and above him the face of the Re'Nuck emerges. What begins as a grin soon twists into a leer, and Apius reaches an hand down, stroking his face roughly. 'Helpless now, eh? Perhaps you will not be such a pest to us any more.'

Apius reaches down again, clenching his hand into a claw. With long, raking nails, the leader of the Animexians gouges into the all-too-yielding flesh of his eyes...

The dreams rage on, a hundred, a thousand, a swift procession of nightmares from the deepest recesses of his mind. These are not thoughts that could have any life except in this circumstance, at this

moment. This is the result of the The Summoning.
This and the many more impacts felt all over Genem.

The Consequences

The sun climbs high above Genem, reaching its zenith, looking down impassively at the only settlement on Noukaria. If it could see, or feel, it would be stunned at the sight that lies beneath it.

The most majestic building crafted by Noukari hands has taken a battering. Although it still stands firm, there are wooden slats lying on the floor, leaving holes in the wall of the construct. The doors lie in the mud. Inside, a few rows of the rustic seating lie broken. Luckily the temple was built to survive. The damage there can be easily fixed.

The same cannot be said about the remainder of the village.

Across the settlement, huts have been left in ruins, roofs and walls crumpled to nothingness by the raw power of the psychic blast. Many were empty, their denizens lending their own efforts to The Summoning. Those that were inhabited now see people standing cluelessly around. They find themselves homeless, victims of an action they wanted nothing to do with.

The scene is the same across Genem - broken homes, broken people. All in the name of the Animex.

***

Ameri looks around, taking in the effects of the catastrophe. She had dared to wonder, to imagine any number of terrible outcomes to this endeavour. But nothing could have prepared her for *this*.

The signs of the damage are everywhere, and Ameri cannot image the sunups of effort and energy it will take to repair. Beside that they will have to arrange all the materials for the task as well. Is there enough will to do it?

She cannot answer that question, not right now. All she can do for the time being is see to her own home. She is no builder, but at this moment everyone is going to have to make do.

It is not long before she sees a crowd gathering behind her. They all bear the same stunned expression. She turns to face the conglomeration, not knowing what she can do to help. All she has is her words. Although perhaps words can do *something*.

The question comes from one sheepish individual. 'Ameri, what shall we do? What happens now?' Ameri shakes her head, knowing she cannot give an easy answer. She speaks clearly, loudly, picking up more listeners from the immediate vicinity. Is this about to turn into a *sermon*? It may be. But there will be more truth shared at this single sermon than all of Apius's efforts put together.

'We stand here in a time of great difficulty. Look around you, at what has happened to Genem. Not many sunups ago we were a town of peace, working with our hands to find the food we eat and build the homes we needed. Our lives may not have been filled with pleasure, or excitement, but we had our duties, our relationships, our friendships. We were building a society where there never had been one before. Such a thing cannot be done easily. But now we have taken a huge step backwards, a setback we *must* endure. That is the important thing right now. It is vital that we all work together to repair everything we held dear in Genem. And do not think of yourselves first – think of those who need help most of all. Everything will be made right in time. If that means sharing a hut with a friend, or giving up some of your usual duties, then you must do so.'

'What shall we do about the Animexians?'

'Their words and their actions have caused incredible damage here. Will they work with us to help us, or will they look after their own? Perhaps. We cannot *count* on them. You must all remember that going forward. While they concern themselves with that which cannot be seen, we must look at what is around us. That has always been the Noukari way. Let that be your focus for now. The Animexians is a matter that we must deal with at a later time.'

'Deal with? What does that mean?'

'I do not know yet. For now, there is plenty to be done. I shall think more on the matter in time.'

As Ameri makes her final proclamation, she is delighted to see the gathering break up into smaller groups, deciding on tasks and setting off to achieve them.

Ameri decides that she has her own important task to see to. Her hut will wait, for now.

***

Heading to the very outskirts, the true scale of the damage is reiterated. Distance from the ceremony seems to have made little difference. Wooden planks lie scattered across the land, and people look out nervously from half-broken huts. She tries to offer a smile, but it has no feeling. She cannot see any injuries as yet, but surely there cannot be so much destruction and no-one wounded or worse. Zerial's hut has not escaped the psychic after-effects of Viarus and his brethren. She can see Olurus sitting on the floor, rocking gently, and she moves to console him.

'Olurus? Are you hurt? Are you all right?'

'*All right!* How can anything be all right again? Look at this place!'

'Yes, Olurus, there is much damage done. But we will rise again. What is done can be undone.'

'How many of us heard it, Ameri? The cry, the scream?'

'We will get over that too, in time. I do not know how many heard it - not all are as attuned as us. I suspect those involved in The Summoning will have suffered most.'

'There is so much damage done. Just look at Zerial...'

Ameri turns to the prone Zerial, body filled with sleeproot to lock up a mind filled with hatred. His head is bloodied, but the wound has coagulated to a sticky red.

'Is he all right?'

'There is no way of knowing. The sleeproot is deep in his system now. He may be fine - he may...'

'He may what?'

'He may never be able to wake again. We are deep into uncharted territory, Ameri. We are unprepared to deal with these events! We cannot...'

'Calm down, Olurus. Of all people, I need you sane and sensible right now. There is too much madness going on around Genem as it stands. Please, I need your strength to add to mine.'

'Yes. Very well. I am sorry, Ameri.'

'Do not be sorry. Simply be yourself and all will be well. We have never been in this situation, but now we find ourselves here we must adapt. I need you to find a healer and bring him here at once. He may be able to tell us more about Zerial.'

'What are you going to do?'

'I am going to stay with him. I will decide what must be done after that.'

'Very well. Thank you, Ameri.'

She nods, and takes a seat on the floor next to Zerial. As she looks over him, concerned, she finally notices the weariness that has settled upon her. What has brought that about, she wonders? The worries of the last few sunups? The confrontations between Zerial, Viarus and Apius? The foul squeal of the Animexians trying to reach their gods? The burden of being looked to for leadership?

Just for a moment, she decides to rest her eyes. Just a moment, no more.

***

The next thing she is conscious of is Olurus gently shaking her back to wakefulness. 'Deria is here, the healer.'

'Good. Very good.' Ameri nods to Deria, who tips her head accordingly.

'This must be him? The famous Zerial?'

'Famous?' replies Ameri. She shakes her head, not liking the direction of conversation. Turning to Olurus, she says, 'Go and see what you can do to help around the village.'

'Yes, Ameri.' He leaves reticently, but follows her command without complaint.

'Just the two of us, eh? Didn't want him to hear what you had to say?' Deria prods knowingly.

'I have nothing to say that Olurus does not already know. And whatever you consider him famous for, rest assured it is an undesired fame.'

'Especially if this is the end result.' Deria replies, kneeling to the floor beside Zerial.

'Is he unconscious?'

'No... well, I cannot be sure. He has been given sleeproot.'

'Sleeproot? Who gave him sleeproot?'

'Olurus said he could obtain some, then I gave it to him.'

'Why would you do such a thing?'

'For his own good.'

'For his own good. *For his own good?* Do you have any concept of what sleeproot can do?'

'It simply allows someone to... rest. Zerial was much in need of rest.'

Deria shakes her head, looking unhappily at the head wound. She pries open his closed eyes, but nothing can be seen but the whites. She lifts a lifeless arm, lets it fall. Then she rounds on Ameri.

'I will explain to you what sleeproot does, and then perhaps you will understand. Our own experimentation on the plant is in its early stages. A simple dose of the root is enough to put a person to sleep for many sunups, during which time they will be completely unwakeable. To the external eye, they may as well be dead. You have seen just how deeply your friend is *resting*.'

'This what what we wanted, needed.'

'There is a side-effect of the plant, though. It is not simply a sleeping draught to be used at will. While the body may be quietened, rest assured that the mind of the individual will be active, far more so than usual. Those we have placed under its influence have woken telling of wild and disturbing dreams. They have been set upon by an unpleasant fear and discomfort for sunups afterwards. This seems to have been affected by external events also – when the rain fell, there were nightmares of floods and drowning. When the sun was high, there were dreams of drought and famine. The mind remains in some way aware of its surroundings, and these feed *into* the mind.'

'So Zerial will be aware of what has been going on around him?'

'In a sense, yes. He may have been having nightmares about you, if you've been here all the time. Or whoever else was standing here, or conversations that might have gone on in his presence. But the worst of it is this wound.'

'It doesn't look too severe.' Ameri replies.

'Physically, no. The wound has shut itself, and seemingly quite quickly, given the blood hasn't fully dried yet. But what is a much bigger concern is what this may have done inside his mind.'

'Inside?'

'Ameri, there's no easy way to say this. Zerial will be having awful nightmares right now, each filled with pain. The physical impact, that moment of agony... right now he will be enduring inner torture.'

'What can we do to wake him up?'

'There is nothing that we can do. Sleeproot has no antidote that we have found. The only thing you can do is wait, and hope that he wakes soon. But I cannot promise that he will be the same person. Such experiences have the potential to change people, and you need to be prepared for that.'

'Prepared? You know I am not his *Wefi*?'

'That is none of my concern. But if you have done this to him, or had a hand in this, then you owe him a debt. Somebody needs to be here when he awakens, a *calming* presence. That might be all you can do for him. Now, if you'll excuse me, there are a lot of demands on my time right now.'

'Of course. Thank you.'

The healer leaves the hut without a reply, leaving Ameri alone with the prostrate Zerial.

Regrouping

At the further reach of Genem, there is a clearing that has already seen too much activity. On the night of First Worship, it witnessed actions from the Noukari the likes of which have never been seen before or since. And now, it has seen the damage of Viarus's deafening mental screech. In the wake of the failed Summoning, there is a scene of utmost carnage.

Viarus is one of the first to rise from the fallen Animexians. He is swamped with a wave of guilt as he surveys his surroundings. Perhaps as the cry emerged from him, he has been least affected. Still, he feels exhausted, leaden-legged. This is all his fault, and he knows it. He let his frustrations get the better of him, tried to rush the ceremony, reached out too hard! But how was he to know that this would be the after-effect? Until now, he had assumed the internal voice to be only that. It was now clear that, given sufficient power and energy, the mental voice could have an effect on the external, and everything within it.

The Re'Nuck is stood next to him, looking in a daze until he notices his companion.

'Viarus! Are you well?'

'We have failed...'

The Re'Nuck's face crumples in thought for a moment as he looks around. 'What have we done, Viarus? Are they... dead?'

'We need to find out. We need to try and wake them.'

'You're right, Viarus. Let us check on our brothers and sisters.'

It takes until the heat of the day for Viarus and the Re'Nuck to work their way round the entire clearing, devoting a small moment of attention to everyone who lies prone. There are moments of joy when some of the Animexians awaken, looking around with stunned eyes. Some smile, glad still to be alive, while others weep at their perceived failure. There will be many more tears to come, as for each of their followers that wakes, there is another who cannot be stirred. Viarus and Apius share the same sadness. But it is Apius who retreats to the centre of the clearing and speaks.

'My brothers, my sisters, today is a dark sunup for all of us. Yet we must remember that no great achievement was made easily. Our religion was founded from nothing. This temple was built from the very ground, with the hands of the most devout of our followers. We have faced obstacles at every turn, and now we face the greatest of challenges. Today we have set out with the clearest of goals. And - I say with a heavy heart - we have failed. Each of us has given everything for The Summoning, and we stand here at the cusp of defeat. Such a thing is not easy to say, nor to accept. But that fact cannot be changed.'

Those gathered draw closer together, stunned but attentive, stepping over what they have yet to realise are the corpses of their brethren.

'Many of you are here to listen to these words. But it is my solemn duty, and my deepest regret, to tell you that the powers that we have unleashed this day have had... unexpected effects. The mental voice has more power than we had ever anticipated, and it has taken some of our brothers and sisters. Some of you may have lost Hasbans and Wefis this day. And for that, I am deeply sorry.'

There are gasps of astonishment, a few screams of despair, the uncontrolled sound of weeping. The Re'Nuck leaves them to have their moment, many of them running round looking for those close to them. Viarus considers himself lucky that he has no Hasban or Wefi to be concerned about - the most important person in his life stands, sombre and proud, within the heart of the clearing.

'Please, brothers, sisters. There is more to be said.' Gradually, even the most distraught of his followers return to hear him. Such is the dedication to the cause. They listen, even if only perfunctorily.

'We have encountered a great setback here today. I promise that tomorrow's sunup sermon be devoted to those that we have lost. You may think that their lives have been wasted, but nothing could be further from the truth. For we *shall* communicate with the gods, and soon. Their sacrifice will be honoured in the greatest way possible – in communion with the Animex! Rest assured that the gods protect them in death. It is crucial that we are not distracted from our course. We will mourn, and give thanks, and then we must move forward. Such is the only way.'

There is no applause, no cheering, no salutation. Many, now free from their obligation to listen to the Re'Nuck, continue their frantic efforts to seek those they love and care for. Apius himself starts the weary trudge from the clearing to his own hut, keen to be alone.

Watching the Re'Nuck go, Viarus takes it upon himself to help those still within the clearing. There is still consolation to be done.

***

When he is finally alone in the clearing, Viarus lets out a heavy sigh. Except that he is not truly alone in the clearing, for frozen eyes still stare at him. He is an oasis of life in a desert of death, and he is the one that caused it all. He breaks down, falling to his knees, allowing tears to come.

No. No, not like this.

He tries to summon some of the courage of the Re'Nuck himself, forcing back the tears. This is not the time to mourn, or castigate. He has done nothing deliberately, he tells himself. But he knows he has a substantial task to carry out, the first stop on his road to closure, to redemption.

He walks into Genem, ghost-like, unseen. The devastation here is to the physical landscape, the buildings fallen and damaged. But they can be fixed, unlike the dead awaiting him in the clearing.

He drifts to the fields and grasps a crude wooden shovel in both hands.

***

Viarus digs.

It is all he can think of. Dig. Dig. Dig. The word becomes a rhythm in his mind, its cadence chiming each time he places the shovel in the ground and spoons out a fresh load of dirt. The mound beside him is growing in proportion. Long ago it exceeded his own height, and now towers over him menacingly. Should it collapse, he could find himself buried. The thought does not perturb him. It is only the task that matters.

Dig. Dig. Dig.

The pit he is working on grows deeper and deeper, and the light of sunup grows weaker and weaker around him. His body is sheened with the sweat of exertion. Once this is done, he knows he will collapse. He knows he will have nothing left. But for now he has purpose and meaning.

Dig. Dig. Dig.

The moons are riding high in the sky by the time he considers this task done. He does now know how he judges it to be done, but something within him says this is the time. He has left an ascent at the far end of the pit, and scrambles up the loose dirt with ease.

This will of course be the worst. Looking into familiar faces turned cold, and unfamiliar faces he will never have the opportunity to know. They will only live within him as corpses. He grabs the first figure he can see, an unfamiliar young woman. His only relief is that her accusing eyes have now closed. Perhaps that will be the case with all the dead.

This woman he drags to the nearest part of the pit and, heaving with all his might, throws her down the soil slope. She lands unceremoniously at the bottom.

For just a moment he wonders if he is doing the right thing. But there is no precedent to go upon. No, he decides, this is fitting. We were brothers and sisters in religion, and so shall be brothers and sisters in death. What else is to be done? Nobody else seems to have considered what should be done with the dead. What might have happened had I not been here, Viarus wonders. The bodies could have been scavenged by wildlife! He could not allow such a thing to happen.

Leaving the first body in its place, he moves to pull the second into its position.

***

By the time the moons begin their descent towards their nadir, Viarus is delighted to have the macabre elements of his task done. He had counted the bodies as he had gone along, tried to index names as best he could. Rejulus, Awala, Niara. 76, 77, 78. So much blood on his hands. What was it that killed them, he wondered? Many had blood caked around their ears and mouths, as though something was trying to *escape* from them. Did he hold such a power within him?

Grabbing his shovel again, he sets about the lonely task of refilling the pit. At least it will not take so long with so many bodies crammed within it.

***

It is sunup by the time Viarus is done, and he wearily sits himself down on the silty floor. So much energy expended, so much emotion burned away. He is suddenly consumed by a hollow feeling.

'You have done very well, old friend.' The voice startles him, but its tones are familiar.

'I have done nothing well, Re'Nuck. All I have done is spent the entire moonrise trying to make up for my failure. Such a thing is impossible, of course, but it gives the illusion, does it not? You could believe that nothing has happened here.'

'I would not want to believe that nothing has happened here. The past does not go away because we simply *bury* it.'

'Do not use that word, Apius. I have buried too many tonight.'

'Apius? Does my rank no longer hold water?'

Viarus emits a long sigh. 'I apologise, Re'Nuck. It has been a difficult time.'

'Of course. I appreciate that. And I appreciate everything you have done.'

'Everything I have done? When we count everything I have done, it makes for poor reading!' Viarus is on his feet, stepping forward menacingly, shovel in hand. 'I have spent the last five sunups teaching a group woefully unprepared for the task at hand. My own mind carried us through a ceremony that fell apart. It was my action that brought death to so many! I have covered myself in no glory. Even laying the dead to rest cannot begin to make up for what I have done.'

'Viarus...'

'It is my time to talk, Re'Nuck. I was never happy with this idea, but I let you persuade me. I doubted that it could be done, but I followed you. I had faith in you. How misplaced that was! I was a misguided fool, and I allowed myself to lead a hundred or more down the same path. And what consequences... fatal consequences, Apius. I will call you that now, because I have *earned* that right. And already you have the audacity to speak of trying again! Do you wish to kill the remainder of your followers, wipe out our religion entirely? How many have to die for you to achieve your ends?'

Viarus finally runs out of steam, throwing the shovel down to the floor and turning away from the Re'Nuck. Apius stands, dumbfounded, seeking some sort of reply.

'Viarus, I would not wish for anyone to die. I am shaken to my core by what has happened. I have barely slept all moonrise, wondering if what I have done was right, whether I acted rashly.'

'But *you* did it! And you would do it again! That remains the fact. I do not know if I can go through this again. Physically, mentally, morally, I think it is wrong.'

'Are you... deserting me, Viarus?'

'Deserting you? As you deserted me, leaving me to clean up the mess your ceremony left behind?'

'That is not a fair accusation.'

'You cannot deny it. And I still believe in the Animex, deeply. But I will not do this again with you.'

'Then we shall have to do it without you.'

'You truly insist on pursuing this path?'

'I will pursue it to the very end.'

Viarus approaches the Re'Nuck. Now they are merely two Noukari, standing face to face.

'This cannot work, Apius. If you cannot see it, then you are delusional. Once you were wise, but now... now you are nothing but a fool.'

'What do you intend to do, Viarus? Are you just going to stand there and menace me, hmm? Or do you want to go a step further? Are you going to strike me, clamber into my mind and hurt me?'

'I intend to do no such thing. But you are lucky that I have not, because the temptation is great.'

Viarus brushes past the Re'Nuck, his ruler no more.

The Mourning

The mood in the Temple of the Animex is sombre, more so than it ever has been. The Re'Nuck stands at the front of the room, the altar separating him from the crowd by the smallest of margins. He is sweating, despite the chill of the morning.

The congregation before him is the smallest that he has seen for some time. Not even one-hundred people sit on the wooden pews. That would have been half the number of the religions at its largest, and many more have not turned up this sunup. This is all that is left of Animexianism, the most loyal.

Mouth dry, he begins to speak.

'My brothers, my sisters, I want to thank you all for coming. It is no secret to look around and see that we have lost many in the last sunup. Some of those are lost to our cause, those that have lost their belief. Some of them have been lost forever, taken from us in the cruellest of fashions. That the gods should take such a toll...'

Apius stifles a tear, his own emotions betraying him.

'We have all lost many dear to us. Hasbans, Wefis, friends and colleagues. But we have also lost many brothers and sisters in our cause, and that is a pain I feel deeply. Our religion has been struck a great blow. But Animexianism does not end here. We are laid low, but not defeated. We may be broken, but we are unbowed. We will return, and our religion will rise to glory once again!'

There is a muted round of applause. Apius does not have to silence it – the patter dies out quickly.

'But that is for another sunup. Today is for us to remember all of those that we have lost. Today is about commemoration, about mourning. It is a dark day, but we must remember all of the best of those we have lost. I would like us all to take a silent moment to remember those most precious moments – the intimacies that we held, the memories that we know shall live forever. Let us bow our heads.'

The silence feels thick within the temple. It seems as though even everyone's breath has fallen quiet. It gives the moment a solemnity that the Re'Nuck knows is needed. He needs it as much as anyone.

'Thank you,' he says with an echo. 'Now I would invite you to come outside with me. Viarus, one of our most loyal...' His voice catches, and the congregation looks up at him eagerly. 'You will notice that Viarus is not here today, but that is because... because he has done a wonderful thing for us. He has buried all of those we have lost, that we may build the most magnificent of memorials right here beside the temple. I do not know if he shall return. He still believes, but he feels this pain more than anyone. But through his work we have a suitable way to remind ourselves of the sacrifices made, give glory to the memories of the fallen. And as such they shall always remain part of us. They gave their lives for it, and they shall continue to follow it.'

There is no movement from those gathered, so it is the Re'Nuck who leads them out of the temple with crisp steps. As he goes, he is glad to hear people rising from their seats, feet shuffling behind him. This is how it should be, he thinks – leaders and followers. He is not beaten yet. Once outside, he leads them all to bow in the heart of the clearing, trying not to picture the vast pile of corpses beneath him. Here he leads another moment of quiet contemplation before speaking.

'Our memorial here shall not be a sculpture, or a building, or a piece of art. It shall be done simply, in a way that speaks to us. I would ask you all, over the next several sunups, to bring an artefact here that meant something to the lost. That way, we shall have the chance to know the fallen in a deeper way than just their name. We shall know who they were, and what their lives meant.'

Apius is first to begin the pile, tossing his ceremonial staff onto the floor.

'This staff has been with me since my first sermon, since

the very earliest days of Animexianism, preaching in this very clearing before our temple existed. This shall serve as the centre of our monument – as they have given to me, it is only fitting I return something to them.' Apius looks longingly at the staff, knowing that any other will never be the same. But now it serves a more important role.

'I have spoken enough. The time for words has passed. Let us depart for our own homes, and consider what honour we wish to give to those we have lost. We will return on sunup.'

The crowd begins to drift away, and many shake the Re'Nuck's hand, or stop to stroke his back or face. Their love for him is still there, despite it all. He accepts these gestures with restraint, until he is finally alone in the clearing. There he falls to his knees, and finally allows his weakness to consume him. Through watery eyes, he watches his tears fall to the soil.

***

He is interrupted by a visitor to the clearing, somebody he had not expected to see. Ameri steps tentatively up behind him, and the still-weeping Re'Nuck turns to face her.

'What do you want, Ameri? This is a dark time for us.'

'It would seem so. But I have already heard whispers you want to try this again.'

'I do not want to. I have to, and I will.'

'Your determination does you credit, Apius. Perhaps it is more than that – stubbornness.'

'It is belief, Ameri. Something you have little understanding of.'

'I believe in much. I believe in the honesty of my fellow man, the integrity of the Noukari, the need to do the right thing here and now.'

'How short-sighted of you. Are you here to try and talk me out of it again?'

'I am here to appeal to your good sense, if you have any.

Just look at what this first attempt has done. How many have you mourned this very sunup? Have you even been deep into Genem, seen the impact your ceremony has wrought? So many are still fixing their homes, and so many lives have yet to be mended.'

'And none of it shall be in vain.'

Ameri shakes her head. 'You mean to proceed with this?'

'I do, with the whole of my heart.'

'Then I give you this promise with the same sincerity – we shall stop you.'

'There is no way to do so.'

'There is, though we do not wish it. Think carefully, Apius. You invite more hurt, more death. Accept that it is *over*.'

Emptied of words, Apius simply shakes his head.

'It is a shame. If you had directed your efforts in the right direction, you could have achieved much,' Ameri says.

She trudges away from the crestfallen Re'Nuck, knowing that she must deliver on her promise if it comes to that.

BENEATH THE VEIL

Life soon enough goes back to normal in Genem, at least on the surface. The signs of the damage are still there, many huts and buildings fixed with only temporary solutions. The field workers go back to their neglected land, the builders return to their constructions, the hunters return to the forests. But beneath it all, the thoughts of what has happened still linger. The workers are missing colleague in their quadrants, the building squads and hunting teams a man light. Will life ever be normal until the scars are all covered? And can they ever be wiped away for good?

Normal is about to be redefined. Hasbans will be paired with new Wefis, tasks will be reallocated, huts will be given to new citizens. Those with the most wisdom and influence will be sorely tested in trying to fix their settlement. But there are now figures with far more power. Those within the ranks of the Animexians look to their Re'Nuck, and the remainder of Genem looks to Ameri. Those lapsed from the ranks of religion look to no-one. They see little future right now.

There is a need for structure, for guidance. The foundations of their people have been shaken to their core, and the need for repair goes far beyond the physical.

***

The dreams continue for Zerial. They have been unrelenting, bombarding his imagination, filling his sleeping mind beyond capacity. They are dreams of pain, dreams of agony, dreams of violence.

A Hiyel crouches low before him, ready to pounce. He turns to run but the creature launches itself at his back, hauling him to the floor, both claws and teeth rending at the sensitive flesh there...

Viarus stands before him, a look of grim determination across his visage. Licking his lips, he reaches out to grasp Zerial's head with both hands, and then the fingers slip through the flesh into the soft matter beneath, each iota deeper bringing fresh waves of misery...

There are hundreds of people standing before him, expressions hollow, mouths slack, eyes blank. They scream at him, scream at the top of their voices. Zerial cannot make out the words. There is only noise, noise that grows and grows until he can feel his ears bleed, a symphony in red...

They are all there – Asha. Viarus. Apius. Olurus. Ameri. Everyone that hurt him. And they are hurting him again and again...

***

The Re'Nuck has set the next Summoning for seven sunups away. The announcement brought little by way of enthusiasm, an unsurprising reaction. It is his own energy, his own belief that will have to carry things this time. Without Viarus by his side, he will have to draw upon his own psychic powers. The deaths still weigh upon him, but they also lend him focus. If they fail again, those losses will have been in vain.

He sits silent in his hut, although his mind is busy. He reaches into his own mind, using the 'channel', as Ameri has called it, to listen in around the village. There are none speaking, or at least none seeking to speak to him. Perhaps that is for the best.

But there is something, some sound that he can feel pushing in from the periphery. He zooms through the mental landscape of Genem, trying to locate the source of this sound. As he closes in on its heart, he realises with a moment of shock what it is.

Screaming.

He breaks the mental connection swiftly. He has heard cries, and shouting, too much in the last few sunups. But this is something else entirely, a sound that comes not just from the mind, but seemingly from every fibre of the being.

Bracing himself, he tunes in his mental ear once again. The screaming only intensifies as he moves closer, and he wonders what could be causing such unearthly noise. As he moves into proximity, it feels as though he is being buffeted by a great gale of agony. It is a dark wind that presses against him. Perhaps it is a warning to keep his distance, but he presses on, step by mental step. When it feels as though he can withstand the hurricane no more, he recognises its source.

Zerial.

He withdraws as swiftly as he can, relieved to emerge from the tornado and withdraw from the inner arena entirely. The rush back to physicality is a jolt, lasting but a moment.

The Re'Nuck takes a moment to assess what has just happened. The last he saw Zerial he produced a similar tumult, but that was a wave of purest fury. This... this was even more harrowing. These were the cries of a man experiencing the utmost torment.

How could such a thing be? Surely no-one could be hurting him, at least not in such a sustained way? What was the source of this bottomless distress?

Nervous to go back to the realm of the mind, at least for now, Apius sets out from his hut.

***

Zerial's hut looks to have sustained minimal damage, although the effects of The Summoning can still be seen. Things outside seem to have been patched up well enough. Apius cannot help but pause before entering. Both times he has been here, he has experienced violence at the hands of Zerial. Will it be the case once more? Still, he has to know what has happened here.

The sight that greets him as he walks in is unexpected. To one side of the hut, Olurus sits uncomfortably against the wall. He is swaddled in furs, and despite the awkwardness of his position he sleeps deeply. On the floor beside him, sleeping every bit as fully, is Zerial. Stepping lightly, he moves to Zerial's side, only now noticing the head wound and the ring of blood there. He must have been injured, but surely that alone cannot explain it? He looks around swiftly. He debates waking Olurus, but doubtless he would see him as an adversary and tell him nothing.

Scanning the room, Apius sees the sleeproot sat on the table. What remains is little more than half.

He must be deeply asleep, Apius reflects. And his dreams must be painful indeed.

Now he knows that he has a course. And perhaps there is a way that he can reach the gods after all.

***

Apius is not relishing his task, but he knows that it is for the greater good. In fact there is a definite irony to the thought – Zerial, his most stoic opposer, unknowingly helping him to reach the gods! But first, he must establish just how far gone Zerial truly is. If the mental barriers the sleeproot places are impenetrable, this will have to be abandoned. But is he can reach into Zerial's mind...

There is much known, and much not known, about the effects of sleeproot. Apius looked into the plant, briefly, to see if it could help his cause, along with many other plants. The drug lives up to its name, but the slumber it brings is dogged with hideous nightmares. Those that wake from it are all too often changed in some way, sleeping uneasily therefrom.

Once the root is swallowed, there is no way to help them. But Apius is not seeking to help.

He enters the psychic landscape once more, finding the source of the scream easily this time. Zerial seems oblivious to him, wrapped up in an unending paroxysm. Whether those nearby can feel his agony pouring forth like a foul wind he cannot tell. Once again he braces against the howling gusts of hell, pushing onwards in spite of the intense discomfort.

Zerial may have been his foe, but even he does not deserve to suffer so. It does not make Apius's task any easier.

Reaching as close as he can stand, Apius launches his own mental assault against the darkness surrounding Zerial. He gathers all his effort and cries 'Zerial! It is I, the Re'Nuck, Apius! I have come to destroy you!'

***

The dreams roll on and on. They never end, seeming to bleed seamlessly from one strand of nightmare to the next. There is no escape for him but to wait for wakefulness.

Asha is laid in bed with him, her warm body pressed against his, the furs enveloping them both. He feels happy, just for a moment, until he feels a squirming sensation across the hand wrapped around his Wefi. He rolls her over, then recoils. The corpse that confronts him is warm, but the warmth does not come from her flesh. It comes from a burrow of insects that have made their home in her stomach, crawling way over his hand as Asha's rotting face looks on...

The image transforms again.

Zerial is standing alone in a clearing. With a shock, he realises that he is stood by the Temple of the Animex. He feels uncomfortably exposed, compelled to take refuge in the temple itself. It is not a place that suits him to be in, but he feels better with a roof above him. There is silence in the temple... no, wait. A faint rustle of clothing, the hint of breath. 'Is someone there?' he asks nervously.

Rising imperious from behind the altar, Apius comes into view. In his hand is a wooden shovel, brandished above his head as though a deadly weapon. He strides forward confidently. 'Zerial! It is I, the Re'Nuck, Apius! I have come to destroy you!'

'Apius! No, no!'

Zerial moves to flee, but as he reaches the door he finds it closed and locked. He pushes against it, but there is no give there. He can feel rather than see Apius advance, crude weapon held high..

***

Beyond this, on the other side of the intangible barrier that separates one mind from another, Apius can pick out the sleeping shouts of his target amidst the tumult. 'No, Apius! Please...' He has never been so pleased to be part of a nightmare. He smiles to himself, his suspicions confirmed.

Yes, there is nothing that can be done to help the dreamer under the influence of sleeproot. Whatever they encounter, in their mind or outside, is converted into the very stuff of their nightmares. The bloody welt on Zerial's head has only allowed more shadows into his dreams, the spectre of pain haunting him each moment. Anyone who reaches into his mind will only add to that.

Which suits his purposes perfectly. He cannot assist Zerial. But by interjecting himself in this way, he can direct the nightmares of his old foe. If he can use his influence to bring them to their greatest pitch, until his mental anguish cannot be ignored by anyone – *even the Animex themselves* – then it may just be possible to reach them.

He leaves Zerial to his nightmares for now, knowing they can take whatever shape pleases him the most.

Opposition

he sunups pass quickly, too quickly, approaching the second Summoning from the Animexians. And with it the prospect of more deaths.

Ameri travels the village all day, stopping and talking to people. Many reactions are hostile. Naturally the Animexians among them are horrified that anyone *should* make an effort to stop the ceremony. It is the Re'Nuck's will. Ameri cannot help but be alarmed at how rote the words sound, the same sentences in the same intonations. It screams of indoctrination.

Not that she finds blanket support from outside the religion. The timidity of her people frustrates her. They look away, muttering weak platitudes. They turn pale at the thought of stirring to action, running from her rather than having a conversation. They react with a fury she wishes they could turn in the right direction, but instead they vent to her. They accuse her of interfering, meddling. Such blindness! Such ignorance!

But thankfully there are those willing to hear her, those who respond with the same passion as she has. By the time the moon begins to rise, she has rallied some fifty individuals willing to come to a meeting of the A'Nockians. She is sharply aware that Zerial will not be there, but his cause is lost. For now. She dares not think beyond that, unwilling to give voice to her own future fear.

***

The next sunup sees the gathering, which Ameri hosts in the A'nockians' hut on the very outskirts of Genem. She has deliberately timed it to coincide with the Animexian sermon that Re'Nuck will be giving far away. This is a pivotal moment. Direct action has gone past being an option and become a necessity. She has drawn these fifty here, and now she must inspire them to action. Olurus has become obsessed with Zerial's state of mind and wellbeing, and one by one the remaining A'Nockians have sought to distance themselves from her. They were thinkers, nothing more.

As the Re'Nuck sermonises on the other side of Genem, the same task falls to her. Only Olurus stands by her side, albeit unwillingly torn from Zerial's side.

The crowd looks uneasy, unsettled. They shift on their feet. They look at each other with veiled glances. There is little conversation, and what there is comes only in snatches. There has been so much uncertainty in their lives of late, and it is up to her to offer them certainty.

'Welcome everybody, and thank you for being here. We have endured a great deal of pain and loss. And the reason we are all gathered here is that we cannot bear to endure such feelings again. Many of us have to date put up with Animexianism, but now that is no longer an option. Their presence has long been an inconvenience. Now they are a *threat*! Their last Summoning took lives, and left us all to mend homes and buildings. Now they propose to do so once again. The time has come for us to stop hesitating. We must no longer look on. This is the time for us to strike. It is not in our nature to fight. But we cannot allow this ceremony to happen again. I have spoken to the Re'Nuck, and he will not be moved. That only leaves us one course of action. We must move against him. We have a few sunups to gather ourselves, steel our courage and prepare for... for combat.'

The word sits uneasily with her, but she cannot lie to her fellows. At the use of the word, there is much mumbling. But at least no-one has left the room, Ameri thinks to herself. They stand stoic.

'This is something that none of us relishes. Our hand is being forced by Apius. We all know the time and place of the ceremony - we have all heard it rumoured. We must be there, and be ready. I am sorry that this must be our course of action, but I will do my duty, as we all must. Thank you.'

Her words have had the desired effect, at least so it seems. The crowd drifts off, and in the end it is only her and Olurus left in the room, staring at each other uneasily.

'I do not know if I can do this with you, Ameri.'

'You, Olurus? Of all people...'

'I must tell you how I feel, Ameri. This is no course of action, even as a last resort. I would rather let them have their ceremony than openly enter into battle!'

'I never had you down for a coward. I always thought that you would follow this to its bitter end.'

'This is too bitter an end. I wanted to join a group that would encourage thought, discussion, change minds with words! We are not fighters, Ameri! I have never wielded a weapon, or even tried to strike a blow. Now you ask us to put together an *army*? Are you a general, a military leader?'

'No, Olurus, I am not. But I am a *leader*! I will do what must be done, that is what a true leader does. I do not run away when things become difficult. That is the difference between me and you.'

'This is madness, you must know that. Are we animals, squabbling like the Hiyel? We are *better* than this!'

'You hide behind your high morals. The end of the matter is that Apius most be stopped, and none of our words have achieved that. This is our only option. You stay with Zerial, Olurus. Hide while your fellows do what must be done. The rest of the A'Nockians have done much the same.'

Ameri moves away from Olurus, leaving him alone in the hut where their group began.

BETRAYALS

Apius strides into the clearing. The impetus is gathering for the second Summoning, and this time he feels success is theirs for the taking. The initial reticence among the congregation is slowly giving way to enthusiasm. They sense a chance to make something from the deaths of those close to them.

This sermon will again focus on those efforts. But he knows that he cannot tell them the *absolute* truth of what will happen. Zerial's unwilling part in proceedings will be a key part of their triumph. He has already seen, first hand, that Zerial will be a far better conduit than Viarus. Viarus had belief, but lacked the raw mental power of his old adversary. The A'Nockians have unwittingly played into his hands by drugging him. The mind is malleable in the state of dreaming. Apius knows he must use this to his own advantage. Would his followers see it this way? He does not think so, but by the time they realise it will be too late. The gods will speak to them, one and all. In the end, that is what will be remembered.

As he reaches the temple, he becomes aware of a figure stood to his left. He turns to face the individual, and is surprised to see Olurus. He looks serious, jaded black circles beneath his eyes.

'Olurus? What bring you here? Has Ameri sent you here once again to try and stop me?'

'Ameri does not know I am here.'

'I see. Your own mission of mercy.'

'You misunderstand my visit, Re'Nuck.'

'Re'Nuck? You acknowledge my title. To what do I owe that honour?'

'We have been... hostile in the past, Re'Nuck. I have not come today in that spirit.'

'Then why are you here, Olurus? My sermon starts shortly.'

'I do not want to see violence engulf Genem.'

'Violence? What is it you speak of?'

'Last sunup, I was at a meeting which... disturbed me greatly. There are many in our village who do not want to see the ceremony happen a second time.'

'This is no secret.'

'But they are willing to act to stop you. Ameri has asked them all to gather weapons, ready themselves for conflict. They will hurt you. Perhaps they will kill you. I do not know.'

'Why are you telling me this, Olurus? These are your own number!'

'I shudder to think of Noukari committing violence on Noukari. I would rather see your ceremony take place than what Ameri proposes.'

'These are strange times, Olurus. I never expected that you would help me.'

'My interest in not in helping you, but in doing what I can for all my fellows.'

'I'm sure your fellows would not look kindly upon this action.'

'They may look on it as they please. I have done what I consider right.'

'Thank you, Olurus. This changes much for me.'

'Do not thank me. Carry out your ritual. Try and succeed this time around.'

His piece said, Olurus leaves Apius to consider his next manoeuvre.

***

Apius seats himself on the altar. How long will it be until his followers begin to arrive? He prefers to take time to consider decisions, but this needs snap judgement. He cannot risk the chance of his ceremony being interrupted. Such a thing would be the end of his efforts. So what to do?

He must move the ceremony forward. And he must be

sure that it is kept quiet. If word goes back to Ameri, then she will act even sooner. It will make things harder, but his hand has been forced.

As the first of his followers arrive, he leaps from the altar, adopting his finest posture of repose. He must not let on his own panic if he is to lead his followers down this path.

***

Ameri sits quietly in her hut. Besides her sits the only weapon she can imagine mustering - a length of wooden branch, fashioned into a cudgel. Most of it she has done with her bare hands. There is blood under her nails, but she cares little for that. There will be more blood than this shed. She tries to picture herself wielding the club, the crash of wood upon skull and bone, the crunch of impact.

It must be done. If it comes to it, it must be done.

Her silence is broken by a figure standing at her door. She starts, taking a moment to recognise him.

'Viarus?'

'I am sorry to disturb you, Ameri.'

She scrabbles back as far as she can, holding her cudgel defensively.

'Please, Ameri. I do not want you to be afraid.'

'Just leave, Viarus. Please.'

'I am not here to hurt you. I only wish to talk.'

'Talk? What do we have to talk about? You have made your views perfectly clear.'

'Much has happened since then. It is... not easy for me to be stood here. I have been thinking long and hard about what to do. This whole business... sits ill with me.'

'What do you want to say, Viarus?'

'I am here to join forces with you.'

'Join forces? After everything!'

'We are all far beyond our comfort zone. We have stood too many times as enemies. But I see now that I have allowed myself to be manipulated, dragged into an untenable situation. I have much to atone for. Whenever I see someone repairing their home, I know it is my fault. Whenever I see a Hasban without a Wefi, that is my fault. Whenever I see mourning faces, the guilt is too much...'

Viarus struggles to bite back tears, and Ameri waits for him to go on. Her initial suspicion is beginning to wane, but she still remains watchful for any signs of deceit.

'I realise now he used me. He used me then, and he wanted to use me once more. I supported him through it all, but I could not make him see that he was *wrong*. And so I come to you today. I have no desire to help him any more. I think that... that he has started to lose his mind. No sane man could pursue this course having seen what he has seen!'

'You have to understand this is hard to believe.'

'But I am genuine - I have shed many tears over the last few sunups for all I have done. If I can stop him trying again, then I will have gone some way towards my redemption.'

After a few tense seconds, she extends her arm and the two of them shake hands.

'Welcome aboard, Viarus. It is good to see that you have seen sense. And there is no need for your guilt, you may rest assured.'

'Thank you for your words, but I am more grateful for the chance to *do* something.'

***

That moonrise, a strange silence descends over Genem. Even the animals of the forests seem to have been quieted, the cries of the Hiyel and the rustling of the Arala in the leaves absent.

And, from a distant spot in the stars, another pair of eyes quietly watch on.

The Second Cataclysm

Zerial lays still, his body and muscle wasting as the sleeproot refuses to relinquish its grip. How long has he slumbered? How long has he dreamed? Time has lost all meaning in the prison forged by sleep. All he can understand are the nightmares, which blend into one another, an unending tapestry. They have taunted him a thousand times with images of his lost Wefi, Asha, her corpse still moving, walking towards him in conflict with all laws of life and death. He can feel the agony stabbed into his mind by Viarus all over again, a shadowy figure laughing at the torment he causes. But worst of all are the dreams filled with the figure of Apius. The Re'Nuck has become his prime tormentor.

And it is now that the image of Apius returns to him. The looming frame stands ten times his own height, and Zerial runs frantically, but Apius strides one to his ten. In seconds Zerial can feel himself being hauled from the floor, held tight behind unbreakable fingers. He tries to escape, even though it means a fall to certain death. That would surely be better than what Apius has in mind.

The fingers close in, oh so slowly, relishing the agony that rips through Zerial. He can hear and feel individual bones break as the pressure grows, and he cries out for help. Ameri! Olurus! The fingers contract further, his own limp and useless arms no help as the digits squash his ribs. He begs for mercy. He begs for a quick death. He begs for it to be over. But Apius grants none of those pleas, tightening his grip a little further, until Zerial can feel his heart give way beneath the pressure...

So much pain, all felt at once...

Apius this time has him tied down, restrained to the floor with a host of ropes and twine. Zerial wriggles, trying to find some form of freedom, but there is no give. Apius is much smaller this time, but his shape is no less cruel. His hands are tipped with cruelly curved nails. He grins as he makes his approach. He shows the blade-like nails to Zerial, running them across his face, not enough to cut but plenty to *confirm just how sharp they are. The first cut comes rapidly, a slash across the cheek, drawing blood. But Apius wants to make him wait. He spends some time with the nails exploring the exposed frame before him, looking at the best places to cut.*

The incisions, when they come, are launched in a frenzy. Apius is a moving knife, the cuts arced and angled to draw the maximum amount of blood. Zerial cries out, cries out as loud as his voice will allow. Why will no-one help him? Asha! Asha! She would always have helped...

The whirl of frenetic activity comes to an end, and Zerial realises he is still alive. It is no relief.

The next wave of cuts is more controlled, as though Apius is attempting to create a masterpiece drawn in lifeblood. There is none of the fury, but much more of method. He is at the mercy of a craftsman whose medium is pain. Each incision brings forth a scream. The carefully chosen slashes feel as though they will never heal. A rasping voice comes from the twisted lips of Apius.

'Beg for help!'

At first Zerial refuses, shaking his head emphatically, but Apius lifts his fury once more at his lack of compliance. The calculated cuts end with a renewed blitz of knife-like fingers, and in bloodied moments Zerial cannot help himself.

'Help! Help! Asha!'

The husky tone of Apius responds to his plea.

'She cannot help you. She is dead, killed by my own hand!'

The pain that lingers on the skin of Zerial is intensified by the pain beneath.

'Olurus!'

'Olurus will not help you. He has turned his back, forsaken your cause!'

'Help! Ameri! Please!'

'Ameri cares nothing for you. She would not help you, even if she could. You are mine, *Zerial.'*

'Anyone! Anyone!'

'Only the gods can save you now!'

Apius draws his bladed fingers together, thrusting downwards with violent force. The seemingly unlimited pain of death comes as a sweet release...

A release that lasts barely a moment...

The next dreams happen too fast for him to take in, but each is a jagged moment of agony. He barely has time to wonder what fresh horror awaits before it is upon him. There are punches and slaps across his face with stone fingers, tube-like digits reaching deep into his throat to scratch at his lungs from the inside, flesh somehow melding with his own and reshaping him into hideous disfigurements, and all the while the misery, the endless stream of agony, shouts and begging...

Ever-present is the face of Apius, twisted into a sneer, wanting, needing to bring pain without end...

He cries, and cries, shouting out to anyone he can think of that might help. The final, desperate scream betrays all that he has ever stood for...

'Animex! Gods, please help me!'

With this very proclamation, the pain ends. And in its place is only a yawning oblivion. No more pain, no more pleasure. Just blackness, and Zerial is contented with that.

***

In a quiet hut on the outskirts of Genem, there is death. The Noukari are unused to death. They have seen little of it, compared to others in the galaxy. Olurus watches Zerial uneasily. The poor man's face has grown pale and wan, his visage sheened with sweat. His body contorts at unnatural angles, movements of arms, legs and head spasmodic. He lets up small whimper, but Olurus knows that under the effect of the sleeproot this must represent of a pain beyond imagining. If only he had known that the drug would bring such nightmares, he would never...

Zerial's body suddenly twists into a rictus, and Olurus is stunned to see the sleeper suddenly sitting up. His eyes are open, but Olurus knows from the empty stare that they see nothing. Instinctively Olurus constructs a mental shield-wall, fearing the worst in this moment. After a pregnant silence, Zerial lets out a scream that is too loud, too powerful, too all-encompassing to emerge from the lips of any of his kind. The sounds knocks him back a step, sending him sprawling.

The noise finally subsides, and when Olurus looks up again he sees that Zerial has fallen flatly back to the bed. He knows without having to look that the nightmare is finally over for him.

In death, a wave of blistering psychic energy blasts from the body of Zerial. Its pure impact sends Olurus flying from the hut, crashing against the wood of the wall and eventually spiralling out of the door. He lands yards away, stunned and confused. But alive, if only due to mental defences.

He know all along that Zerial had power, but he had no idea that it could be released so potently and so swiftly even in his deepest sleep.

***

The ground of Noukaria shakes, bringing the simple buildings of Genem to the floor, wood cracking and splintering to kindling. The quaking earth is torn asunder, cracks and fissures opening to reveal gaping pits. The very sky itself joins in the tumult, opening with a dark rain that lashes down, the rage of the sky unleashed. Lightning cracks, casting the whole darkened scene in stark shades of actinic blue. The lashing rain draws welts, sometimes blood. The growing cover of the cloud gives the impression of shadiest moonrise, only intermittently broken with flashes from the sky, revealing small, jagged hells.

Many flee into the forest around them, seeking refuge there. They find none. The violence of lightning crashes into the height of the trees, burning them to blackness or sending them crashing. The creatures of the forest are forced to flee, and the Noukari darting there find themselves dodging tumbling boles. Scuttling creatures are crushed in blasts of blood beneath the fallen trunks.

There are screams as Noukari rush from their homes,

trying to reach some kind of safety. Some dash aimlessly for other huts, trying to press themselves inside as unwelcome visitors. Others simply stand watching the scene, paralysed by fear. They are static islands in a swelling ocean of movement. It is a blend of panic and stillness, two different kinds of madness meeting head on.

***

As the wave of energy subsides, Apius finally opens his eyes. He relished the pain he was able to cause Zerial – is it wrong to admit such? Perhaps, but Zerial has wrought his share of pain upon him. Yet he had never guessed at the power Zerial would be able to unleash. Thankfully this time around he had a greater understanding of the forces he was dealing with. He has managed to deflect the majority of the power upwards. Even Viarus could never have produced such a masterful effort.

In taking a first look around the clearing, he can see that the effect of his efforts have still been profound. There are cracks and chasms in the very ground, which it seems most of his followers have managed to avoid. Those who have fallen will never be seen again. There are numerous planks in the temple which have started to bow and splinter, but the proud structure still stands. The Animex themselves would have wished it so. There is one fallen tree, which splits the clearing in two with its vast trunk. He can see one arm emerging from beneath it, and knows that at least one more follower is lost to him. The others?

They stand in surprise, in shock, a few with slack smiles that demonstrate some sort of delight. They have done it. Apius knows it, and he can see the fact dawning upon the rest of them. Their efforts and their faith have been rewarded. The Animex must have heard such a cry.

He still says nothing, allowing his flock to gather themselves. Instinctively, without any speech at all, they draw closer to him. This gravitation sees them all soon enough ready to hear him. Surely it is a moment too momentous for him even to do justice to. But what will the books say of him, the silent leader at the greatest moment of his triumph? No, this *deserves* words.

'Brothers, sisters, we have achieved what all too many thought was impossible today. We have conjured a call that even the Animex cannot ignore. You will be remembered as the first of many to speak to the gods themselves!'

As Apius again falls silent, he becomes aware of just how deep the stillness and quiet around him is.

Then the silence is shattered by distant cries of anguish, cries of pain.

THE FIRST WAR

The shock around Genem is soon replaced by fury. Ameri is the very avatar of it as she emerges from her hut, much of which has fallen around her. Only the door and the semblance of two walls remains. The roof collapsed inwards above her, and only her quick reflexes ensured her survival. Drawing her arms above her head to shield her skull, presenting her back to the tumbling beams, she is sore and bruised but nothing worse.

As she steps outside, the true scale of the devastation strikes as a physical blow. Her hut is one of many struck low, little more than loose conglomerations of splinters. There are shattered cracks in the ground, which look impossibly deep at a simple glance. There is dust everywhere, and a smell of burnt wood taints the air. She picks up beneath that the metallic tint of blood.

They did it, she realises. They did it before they were ready! They did it secretly, so that they could not be stopped!

Her anger rises, white hot, spilling from her lips as she screams. It is a cry of frustration that stops all of those within earshot. Her hatred has never been so raw, her rage so untempered.

This is the end of it all. This is the time.

She grabs a jagged length of wood that was once part of her hut and dashes from the surrounds of her broken home.

***

There is an atmosphere of celebration in the clearing. The overriding sense of success is so that no-one even considered injuries or deaths among them, although they have undoubtedly happened. There are hugs, handshakes, congratulations from one to another. Apius warmly greets each one of his followers, proclaiming theirs a key role in their success. In truth, there was no role more vital that his own. Except perhaps that of Zerial, but the Re'Nuck doubts that his old adversary will be able to enjoy the acclaim.

Many have already started work on the temple, doing their best to fix the damage done to both exterior and interior. Broken but unbowed, so much like their very religion.

Apius looks to the now-clear skies, and knows that they have been heard. The slight whistle of the wind is the only sound as he breathes in his own achievement.

No. There is another sound. Far away, but growing louder all the time. A rumbling, discontented sound. A sound that strikes a note of fear into his heart.

'Brothers! Sisters!' he cries. All eyes turn to him, but he does not know what to say. 'They come!' is all he can muster.

The warning comes barely in time. Rows and rows of their fellow Noukari burst into the clearing, each wielding some manner of crude weapon: a shovel, a misshapen club, a wooden pitchfork. They have a glare in their eyes, and Apius cannot help but wither before the expression. He has never seen such from his fellow man and woman.

They look like an army, he thinks.

Behind him the brothers and sisters of Animexianism have gathered, each as grimly rapt with the scene as Apius himself. Once all of this incoming force have moved into the clearing, they pause, an action in response to the signal given by their leader.

Ameri.

Apius looks at her, his body filling with every bit as much as cold hatred as she holds. Her constant opposition to the truth, to the gods, has gone on long enough. Their eyes meet, two baleful gazes that remain unbroken even as they stride forward to the centre of the clearing. There is no movement but the two of them. Once they have closed, they begin to circle one another, two hungry predators in a dance that can only end in death.

'You should not have come here, Ameri. This cannot end well for you.'

'On the contrary, false Re'Nuck. I should have come much sooner.'

'False? I have done nothing false! I have pursued only the truth.'

'You have pursued your own agenda, and the gods you *created*. I care not if this ends well for me. But be sure that this ends now.'

'I would have it no other way. Ameri. I only hope I get the pleasure of killing you myself.'

Ameri's eyes close a fraction further, and with a roar she launches herself forward. The unbalanced club is awkward in her hands, and the blow launches her far past the elusive Apius.

But this action is enough to ignite the incendiary atmosphere that has been threatening to explode. Rivalries and suspicions that have boiled beneath the surface are finally ready to be unleashed.

The warriors of Ameri and A'Nockianism dash forward, war cries on their lips, ready to dispense death with their blunt weapons.

The followers of Apius spring forward in response, unarmed, but equally ready to fight in the name of their leader.

Ameri lifts the club awkwardly once more, but before she can ready for another strike she feels the lash of a kicking foot crash into the small of her back. She tumbles forward, face down in the wet soil. Mud gathers in her eyes, her mouth. Spinning onto her back, she rolls out of the way of Apius's descending fist. He curses as Ameri rolls to her feet.

'Not bad, for one with a liar's heart!' he shouts, but knows that he is too late to be heard. All around them, in the heart of the clearing where it all began, the two sides of the Noukari enter into combat.

***

Warfare is never a beautiful thing. Perhaps those commanding their forces may see the deployment of their tactics as a thing of beauty. Maybe even the martial skills of the trained warriors involved could be admired. The weaponry may be finely-crafted, glorious objects to be admired.

The conflict between Noukari and Noukari has none of these things.

This is warfare at its ugliest and most brutal. There is a purity of cause and a bursting hatred prompting men and women to do whatever it takes to best their foes.

Viarus, in the heart of the A'Nockian vanguard, has never seen anything like it. Adrenaline pumps in his veins. Fear drives him to action. Raw fury drives his hand as his shovel crashes into the face of the first Animexian he comes across, the flat wooden face stopping his charging foe with blunt force. The man crumples to the dirt, a bloody gout streaming from his nose. Without hesitation, Viarus swings the shovel downwards. He wants to hurt. He *likes* the blood. The flat connects again with the already broken nose. There is a rewarding crunch, but Viarus is not done. He smashes the face viciously, time and time again, until the wood is stained red on brown.

So much hurt, so willingly caused, on those who used to be his brothers and sisters. But no more than he has already caused.

'Rest in peace, Juvus,' he whispers to himself before moving deeper into the conflict.

***

Ameri lifts herself to her feet as Apius seeks to press in, keen to press the advantage. Ameri is slowed, but more determined than ever to destroy her foe. She swings out clumsily again with the club, missing Apius and sending herself spinning on the spot. The Re'Nuck does not miss the opportunity – his punch lands right on her chin. Ameri reels. Ameri rocks.

Ameri holds her feet.

Apius moves in for a second strike, but Ameri ducks

beneath the blow this time. Still holding her club in her hands, she jabs the blunt end into his stomach. Apius doubles over. Ameri rises, looking for a finishing blow. The downswung club misses Apius by the smallest of margins as the Re'Nuck falls backwards, his only defence. Ameri tosses the club aside and launches herself at her grounded enemy. The club has helped her none – perhaps hand to hand combat will afford her more luck.

Their conflict remains private. No-one else would be willing to step into the battle between their two leaders. All around them is chaos, but it is nothing more than periphery to their personal war.

***

Viarus allows his hateful expression, taking his revenge on those he once called brother. Piapus looks at him pleadingly, not understanding why.

He always was a fool.

The shovel crashes into the side of his skull, which is instantly reduced to a red ruin by the force of the blow. As Piapus falls, Viarus lands another blow on the backstroke. The squelch of ruined bone and grey matter does not move him.

A body lands heavily on his back, and Viarus turns to try and shake the grappler behind him. The figure clings on tenaciously, and so Viarus does what comes instinctively.

He falls limply backwards.

The figure beneath him has nowhere to go, landing heavily beneath him. Still the hands of the stranger close around his neck. Viarus tries to get to his feet.

The hands tighten.

Viarus attempts to get his own fingers beneath the iron grip of his combatant. The digits do not give.

The hands tighten further.

Viarus can feel the breath escaping him. His lungs start to burn. The air is about to run out, and his life with it.

Another figure looms above him, this one lashing

downwards with bare fists at Viarus's assailant.

The hands loosen.

Viarus rolls away, choking.

The Animexian that helped him looks down in horror, realising that he has just assaulted one of his own kind, that Viarus is now their common enemy.

The two of them round on him, but still his odds are better than they were moments ago. Gripping his shovel, he takes a step forward into a battle stance.

***

Ameri lands on top of Apius, who instantly tries to crawl away from beneath her weight. She straddles him, pinning him to the softened soil. She scratches at his face, his eyes, drawing dark red trails of blood with her bare hands. Apius tries to defend himself, but can go nowhere.

In a final, desperate act of violence, she presses her nails down direct into the soft flesh of the fear-filled eyeballs of the Re'Nuck.

Apius grips at her forearms, attempting to relieve the pressure, but Ameri will not give. His desperation is no match for the raw cruelty that now fills her.

He can feel the nails breaking through the tender surface of the eyeball, and he cries out in terror, realising that in moments he will be blinded.

He scrambles around, reaching for anything, a stone, a piece of wood, anything that he might strike her with. The only thing he can grasp is a handful of mud, which he flings into her face. The moment of shock is enough for him to roll away, his eyesight marked by red at the edge. He cries out, giving voice to his raw frustration.

The scream that escapes him is mental and not physical, and it is only this that drives Ameri back even slightly. She grips her ears with bloodied fingers, trying to block out the horror of the sound.

So embedded have they been in their physical conflict,

both have forgotten their own mental capabilities. Whatever damage has been done to his eyes, Apius is not impeded even slightly in this battle. He can reach into her mind using his inner eye, and reach he does.

In his time torturing Zerial, he has grown used to the infliction of pain, the infliction of fear. And he can feel that first familiar glimmering of terror within Ameri now.

He plans to use it to his advantage.

***

The screech reaches into another mind not far away. Viarus is almost floored by the mental squeal of agony, and he has to maintain his defence in the face of a barbarous attacker, determined on clawing at him with bare nails. His opponent inflicts a deep gouge in his cheek. The pain is what brings the external world back into focus. The handle of the shovel shoots upwards, outwards, not as effective as the flat head but enough to give him a moment's respite. With a yard or two between them now, Viarus is able to swing the improvised weapon. A satisfying crunch follows. The motion vibrates through the wood all the way to hands and arms. The enemy, once his friend, falls prone. Dead or unconscious, it does not matter for now. He has the freedom to think for the first time.

And he knows he must direct those thoughts against his former master.

He strides forwards to the pair fighting a titanic battle in the middle of the arena of warfare. To an unknowing viewer they may look like the calm eye of the storm, but Viarus knows far better.

***

The battle manifests itself swiftly, the exterior melting away to allow the inner focus. The mind can create any landscape within its imagination, or within any other imagination, given sufficient power and skill. Ameri tries to fight the invading force within her, the arrow given the name of Apius. But his power is too much. She had no idea that his channel had grown so strong. The mental landscape, usually so peaceful, is instantly transformed into a tumult. The land that was once so solid beneath her feet quakes, great rents being torn in its surface. Fire springs as if from nowhere, sourceless, reaching out for her with inferno fingers. She ducks, runs, but the constant feeling remains with her of being herded into a corner. She can hear a wave of cruel laughter, and looks up to see Apius himself. Or at least the resemblance of Apius – he is painted in black, and has wings attached to his shoulders, a grotesque bird-creature. He stands atop a towering pillar of rock, far clear of the catastrophe developing beneath him. Ameri wonders how she can defeat him.

But she knows that she cannot.

That is until another figure runs past her, braving the fire and the breaking earth to launch forward at Apius. This shape is winged too, but painted a paler shade of grey as it ascends. She thinks for a moment that she recognises the figure...

Viarus?

The two bird-shapes come together in a melding of flesh, a ball of violence that tumbles uneasily towards a chasm in the earth. As they crash towards landing the abyss suddenly heals itself, and the chaos all around her dies. She tumbles to the floor in both relief and exhaustion.

Death has been so ready to claim her.

Perhaps it still shall.

***

The cold black eyes of Apius meet the cool grey eyes of Viarus. Apius's mastery of the mental realm has grown, without question, but Viarus has spent his time exploring the power of his own mind as well. The stare is locked until the two of them can bear the stillness no longer.

Aggression explodes between them.

Apius lashes out with a taloned hand, and Viarus ducks below it. He punches forward with his own curved claws. Apius moves quickly backwards, escaping evisceration by the thinnest of margins. A trickle of blood appears on his stomach, mirrored on the end of Viarus's bladed nails.

'You are my master no more, Apius. To think how I used to revere you, look up to you.'

'You still should. That way I may not have to destroy you.'

'Destroy me? You do not have the power. This madness ends here, Re'Nuck.'

The derogatory use of the title spurs Apius into a fresh assault, a flurry of punches and kicks. He has the appearance of a whirlwind, the movement never stopping for a moment. Viarus is equally sinuous in his response, raising arms and legs to produce one block, one parry after another. The dance of death that is carried out between them is dazzling. There are strikes and counter-strikes, grunts and bruises, but nothing conclusive between the two.

Apius lands a punch on Viarus's chin, trying to follow up with a flattening kick. Viarus rolls with the movement of his fall, pirouetting away from the kick. His own slash rakes the cheek of the Re'Nuck, who howls in pain, grasping at the arm that caused the injury and wrenching Viarus to the floor. The stomp intended to crush the skull of his foe is dodged.

Ameri can only watch on, rapt, such smooth and intentional violence unknown to her. Surely nothing can separate them?

That is until the entire mental landscape melts away. The transformation happens in an instant. One moment they all stood on solid ground, the next there was nothing but air beneath them. They all tumble, tumble, tumble, their screams mingling together...

And then the entire mental realm is gone. The three of them are back in their bodies, back in the clearing, back in the real world.

Yet the world is as they have never seen it before.

The Last War

The conflict has ground to a halt as Apius, Viarus and Ameri drag themselves to their feet. The shock of the wrench back to reality still has not fully settled. All around them, where a war was being fought, there is no movement at all. Their friends, their fellows, have all frozen.

And, in their midst, four silver-clad figures share the same sense of stillness.

Ameri watches closely, and they convey no emotion whatsoever. Their sense of stillness is nothing but discipline. She dares to reach out with her mind, just for a moment, but finds her approach met by an unbreakable wall of metal.

Who are these beings that stand among them? And what is the strange construction that casts a vast shadow behind them?

For a moment Ameri is confused, but then remembers what the object reminds her of. The seeding pods in the drawings... the source of their creation...

The door to the vessel is open, disgorging more of the silver aliens that stand in their midst. And they are followed by a figure even more impressive.

The form looks something like the Animex themselves, sharing the same gauntness and rakish height. But there the resemblance ends. The shape is swathed in voluminous robes of blue, produced to a quality far beyond what the Noukari could achieve. The face is old, incredibly old. Ameri is transfixed by the visage. It is not weak, nor feeble, but the eyes have undoubtedly seen much. Much of everything – pain, joy, despair.

And now, they are tinged with disappointment.

Sweeping imperiously into the heart of the clearing, flanked on either side by its shining companions, the being looks over the dead, the injured, the unwounded with the same disdain.

Ameri has to resist the urge to fall to her knees. This may not be a god, but it is unquestionably one of their creators.

The Animex.

The silence is utter until some begin to fall to their knees, debasing themselves before god or creator. They see it differently, but their emotions are much the same. She realises this at the same moment as everyone else. Right now, their differences mean nothing.

They are in the presence of majesty, of the greatest power and wisdom they have ever encountered. The Animex's first words will never be forgotten.

'To arms.'

***

Apius weeps openly, uncontrollably. He is stood in the presence of a god! His message was heard by the celestial beings that created them! He falls to his knees, but cannot prostrate himself any further. He cannot pull his pain-filled eyes from the sight of the holy being, which looks around the clearing. Is there disgust in that expression? As well there should be, given the blood of the Animexians that has been shed! His joy doubles as he realises what this sole Animex has come here to do.

He has come to praise Apius for all he has done. He is here to condemn those who stood in his path, perhaps to kill them, exile them. This will be the moment of his complete triumph, the ascendancy of the Re'Nuck. He can barely see the god and his angels through his moistening eyes.

But he hears the words perfectly clearly.

'To arms.'

Yes! Strike them down! Destroy those who have refused to believe in your godhood!

At this proclamation, the silver-garbed figures begin to move. They swiftly draw something the likes of which Apius has never seen from their belts – but immediately he senses this is something that harnesses *destruction*. They wield it as their enemies have held their clubs and shovels – with deadly intent.

The figures move crisply to the edges of the clearing, a formation that is clearly practiced given their precision and timing.

Then lightning barks from their very hands.

The implements they hold explode into a cacophony of life, spitting electricity into the midst of the silenced Noukari. Those first few struck have no time to react, no time to scream, not even the time to register life turning to death.

Apius watches in horror as the soldiers move inwards, closing their hellish net, casting actinic agony all around them as they go.

That horror grows with the second realisation.

They are striking down only his followers.

Animexian after Animexian is transmogrified from flesh and bone to mere explosions of blood subsumed by the hungry soil. The faces of the loyal fall as they realise these shining angels are in fact their harbingers of destruction.

Half of his religion is extinct by the time any of them have the chance to run, but they only move closer to their deaths, giving these strangers the opportunity to destroy them at closer range.

The web has caught them all.

There is no mistake, only cold precision. This was something that was decided before their arrival. There is no spontaneity, only premeditation.

This is what the Animex wanted all along – to come here and *wipe them out*. The last of their number, poor Akaris, runs and runs, but each time he turns he is face to face with one of the metal-bound warriors. They are toying with him, and Akaris knows that death has come for him, hoping only to prolong his life by seconds more.

Soon enough, he has no seconds left.

Apius has been weeping the whole time, although the reason for the tears has changed. Now he lets out a cry of anguish, both physical and mental, at this denunciation of all he has built.

The scream is cut short by the merest of thoughts from the Animex, an easy reflex that belies huge psychic potential. Apius is silenced, his tongue frozen in his mouth. The stare directed at him by the majestic figure is warning not to repeat the action.

Now the warriors of the Animex close in around him, a glimmering noose closing around his neck.

***

Apius can barely see the approach of his god through bleared eyes. His crying is uncontrollable, endless. He could not find a way to stop if he tried.

Two of the silver warriors step aside to allow the Animex to stand directly in front of his greatest worshipper. He looms over the kneeling form of Apius.

'You wished so much to speak to me, *Re'Nuck?* You would hurt, kill so many just to hear what it is I have to say? I am here, and I bid you to listen. I bid you all to listen, and remember these words!'

None reply. None dare respond to the booming, mesmerising voice.

'I have watched you since day one. You seem so ready to forget so much. The seeding pods that carried you told so much of the story, yet you have preferred to fabricate your own.'

As the Animex looks around the clearing, there are suddenly none willing to meet his steady stare. He continues regardless, knowing that they are listening well enough to him. Their shame is testimony to it.

'At first, I was pleased with your progress. You were the simplest form of life when you arrived, but you quickly grew and developed. Before long you had a working civilisation here, and I believed that things would all be well. My children were making their own way.'

Apius's head has fallen completely to the soil, his tears mingling with the wet dirt beneath. He does not want to hear the words, but there is no way to ignore them. This was what he wanted, once...

'Until this.' The Animex points at the temple, the vast building that dominates the clearing. 'I allowed this to pass, because I believed that as a race you were intelligent enough not to let this grow out of hand. I thought that you would soon enough see the light, and this concept of religion would die out. I will say this now, and say it clearly. I am no god. None of my fellows are gods. We are beings much like yourselves. We have wisdom, intelligence, power. What would we want with religion, even if we *were* gods? Do you think your prayers would mean anything? I have heard it all, and as I stand here, I am *embarrassed* to call myself your creator. I stand here only because I have to prevent a war, to stop the complete annihilation of this settlement!'

The raised voice fills the clearing utterly.

'None of you are innocent. The growth of this religion is at each of your feet. This ends, and it ends now. I had hoped that you would be able to end such a thing yourselves. It is disappointing to see your children fail you so.'

'And you, Apius.' The steady gaze falls upon the Re'Nuck. 'You are the worst of all. Your followers played their part of course, those who filled the temple to hear your false words, those who flocked to you seeking something more than building a society! Not exciting enough for you, Apius? You appointed yourself a title and set about building this... nonsensical... religion of yours. Think of the time, the energy, the efforts of your people that you have wasted! Consider all the blood already on your hands, so many of your fellows lying in the ground because of your actions, your desperate need for our approval! You shall find none, Apius. You will find only our disgust.'

Sejurus nods to one of the silver-bound figures next to him, and the weapon in his hand and held level, aimed dispassionately at the back of Apius's temple.

'Animexianism dies with you. I will stand no repeats of this development, no martyrs in this cause. You have already seen what happens.'

The sound of the single gunshot crashes through the clearing, more emphatic that any shot before it, and Apius's prone body falls to the dirt unceremoniously. He will receive no ritual, no funeral – just a cold death at the hands of his deities.

And his religion lies dead with him.

***

Sejurus shows no remorse at the action, without hesitation gesturing for his warriors to fall back. 'This war ends here. And we will not stand for any more wars among you! We created you to be beings of intelligence, of thought, of great psychic potential. And now look at yourselves! Like common animals, lashing out with bare hands and grasping weapons! This is a disgrace to what you are. I may as well be looking at the simple animals of the forest that surround you.'

Sejurus nods to the warriors, now stood at a distance of several feet.

'And so today I make a proclamation. And it is one that will change your future forever.'

The Noukarta

s a fascinated crowd watches, the twelve that attend to Sejurus slowly remove their helms. With a hiss of air, the faces are revealed, and a gasp emerges from all gathered.

Their faces are exactly the same as their own - Noukari. Nothing but Noukari.

'Look upon them, one and all. Born from the same source, but brought up so differently to yourselves. The Noukarta.'

The dozen step forward in unison, menacing, now flanking the Animex as he speaks. The resemblance to the Noukari themselves is striking, but on closer inspection the differences are there. The facial expressions vary, the mouth downturned slightly in a display of aggression, perhaps even hatred. The skin is more grey than white across the visage. And the body language is that of a predator, a master of its destiny in life and conflict. Their readiness says that they could easily make a mockery of the Noukari's primitive efforts at warfare. The fiery weapons in their hands could slice down any of their number before they could get close enough to inflict even the slightest damage.

'The Noukarta are are bred and built for war, for conflict. I shall be leaving two of my warriors here, a pair of my very finest. Uxurus and Leonis will be my representatives here, keeping watch over you as the Noukari move forward. They shall be defenders if they are ever needed, arbitrators should they be required. And their weapons shall remain with them. But, rest assured, they do not need them to dispense death. They are more than trained in other means of warfare.'

Uxurus and Leonis step forward, their eyes not even shifting from a blank stare. They have no interest in all of the sights arrayed before them in the clearing.

'So it is done. Now, there are two of your number I would speak with. Viarus and Ameri, I bid you to come forward.'

***

Ameri hears her own name, and feels a sense of terror at having to step forward. She emerges from the crowd, conscious of the blood still on her fingernails, the shame that she has brought upon herself in losing herself to violence. She sees Viarus stepping forward with similar unease. The two of them stand before their creator nervously, and Ameri is surprised to feel Viarus slipping his hand into her own. She draws strength from the unexpected contact.

'Ameri, I am the most disappointed in you. I have witnessed you from the earliest days of your life, and you could have been something special, something great. But there is some factor within you that has held you back. I know not what it is, but it has led you to this very point today. You may stand here before me, the very picture of a warrior-woman, but this action has come too late. You knew the truth all along - you held the truth *in your hands* - and yet you did nothing. You shared it with a few that you considered to be safe. You spent so much time talking, talking, considering what things might *mean* when the answers were so obvious! I had considered you one of my brightest prospects, but you have proven many times over that you are not ready for a position beyond that which you have now. Consider what you might have been as you look forward. You may return to your people now.'

The words leave a hole in Ameri, shattering her sense of self. Unsteadily she lets go of Viarus's hand and returns to her place in the crowd.

Sejurus nods down to Viarus, and Viarus is the first among the Noukari to meet his eyes steadily. The eyes there are serious, compassionate, thoughtful, but remain haunted with something else.

'Viarus, I have considered your actions for a long time. I

watched you at the heart of Animexianism, helping to begin that because of what you believed in. You had faith, and you pursued that faith. But what impressed me most is that you realised that you made a *mistake*. When you first tried to reach us, you saw the cost, and you stepped aside. You looked at what had happened, and you were rational. That is a sign of wisdom - something that has been sorely lacking in this farce. You were not too proud to admit what you had done, and you did what you thought was right to mend it.'

'What are you trying to say, master?'

The Animex looks down, almost stunned to be interrupted. No other has dared to speak in his presence. For the first time, he smiles.

'You also have bravery, Viarus. This much I cannot deny. And that is another quality that is important in a leader. From hereon, Viarus, I am appointing you the ruler of this settlement. You have done much wrong, and you have worked to atone. This will serve you well in the future. And so I am appointing you as A'Nock, the true and single ruler of this civilisation. The choices you have made and the psychic potential that you have make you the perfect candidate for this.'

'Thank you, master.'

Viarus withdraws respectfully, stepping backwards with head bowed.

'The remainder of you! I expect you all to abide by this proclamation. Civilisation must be built, and religion must be forgotten. I hope to never have to return again to ensure you are on the right path.'

His piece said, the figure turns sharply and heads back to the metal vessel that he debarked from, ten silver shadows in tow.

NEW WAYS

Within the space of a few sunups, Genem is almost unrecognisable, both in look and outlook. At the very edge of the village, where its most majestic building once stood, now is nothing but an empty clearing. It is a place that holds many scars – some literal, some mental. In keeping with the tradition that its A'Nock began, Genem has buried its dead beneath the soil. In this way they may give rise to some sort of new life.

The temple itself has been torn down, one piece of wood at a time, by those who never gave their allegiance to Animexianism. The wounds are too raw in the exponents of the old religion, a way of life that their gods told them to forget.

Except they are not gods, and they never were. They were just beings, beings of vast power, but nothing more. Those who refused to believe have been vindicated, while those who followed are forced to live with the shame of their mistakes. None gloat, none remind them, but it marks them deeply nonetheless.

The materials from the temple have been used to help build their civilisation. In the heart of Genem, a grand house has been built which from now on will be the abode of the A'Nock. Next to that, one on either side, are two more modest homes. Yet each of these small spaces causes a ripple of unease among the Noukari.

For these are the home of Uxurus and Leonis, the Noukarta. And they are truly a breed apart.

***

Viarus looks around his luxurious home, not sure if he is deserving of the location or the title that hangs upon him. To be given such a role directly by the Animex themselves is a great responsibility. And what does it mean to be an A'Nock? Viarus wonders for a moment if Apius was swallowed by the same doubts as Re'Nuck, but he knows that the answer is no. Apius let the title go to his head, cloud his judgement, lead him to poor decisions. Viarus knows he cannot do the same.

He has turned the words of the Animex around many times, and he realises the importance of mistakes. He has made many of them, and so have the whole of the Noukari. Those who allowed themselves to be led – himself included – made a mistake in putting their faith in Apius. Those who stood against Apius made the mistake of letting it grow. Asha made the mistake of opposing Animexianism alone. Apius made the mistake of creating First Worship and the Summoning.

So many mistakes, so much blame. Something they all must live with.

But the mistakes they have made so far give them the chance to take stock, look at what they have, figure out a better way forward. He has already acknowledged his mistakes, and even more so *forgiven* himself. The errors of the past are already made. The actions of the future are yet to be decided.

This will be what leads the new ways for their people. There is no absolute right and wrong, only good intentions and positive actions. Mistakes are inevitable, a part of life. Rectifying them and learning from them is what is important.

The new A'Nock has yet to address his people, a conscious decision. Too many sermons, too many rousing speeches have been made in the short history of Genem. They have been nothing but agitators, precursors to the violence that exploded among them. As a leader, there is no need for him to address his people, if the people are doing well enough.

That does not have to mean that he is inaccessible, however. He intends to be there when he is needed. When individuals need advice, when groups need help, when Hasban and Wefi need to repair their relationships. A good leader does not make everything his business, but he can deal with everything when it is necessary.

Perhaps that is where both Apius and Ameri made their greatest mistakes.

With a sigh, he makes his first resolution. He moves through the large house, goes to the door, and swings it open. He will not lead from behind a closed door - if his help is wanted, anyone may come through the door and get it.

The open door begs another question - there is one discussion that must be had before he can truly consider himself any kind of ruler. Stepping outside, he decides it is as well done now.

***

In the house of the A'Nock, Viarus looks steadily at the two Noukarta. He requested that they come to him without their armour, their silver second skin, so he may truly see them this time. He does not want to talk to a being that seems to have no face, no eyes, no mouth.

'Welcome to Genem, brothers. It is a pleasure to meet you both, at least in more fortunate circumstances.'

'Thank you, A'Nock. My name is Uxurus, and I have been designated as speaker for the Noukarta.'

'Very well. Then it is well that we should speak. Does this mean that... Leonis will not speak?'

'Only in the most extreme of circumstances. The way of the Noukarta is that leaders speak and their subjects simply *do*. It is the way of military discipline, a code for warriors. I doubt you would understand.'

'I understand leaders must be wise, or else they will drive their followers from the cliff also.'

'A'Nock, I am glad that you have summoned us that we may speak. But I am no philosopher. My thoughts and actions lie elsewhere.'

'Then let us come to the point. I know nothing of your kind. I am pleased to see that you have a resemblance to us beneath your armour, although you are obviously superior physical specimens.'

'That has come at a price of its own.'

'What do you mean?'

'Our masters told us of your powers, the psychic potential within you. Such a thing has been bred out of us - mental strength traded in for physical strength, perhaps.'

'Interesting this should be the case.'

'That makes us less brothers than you would think. Perhaps we are more cousins.'

'If the greeting suits you better. Although I would prefer that our differences were played down.'

'Such a thing would be a denial. At a glance it is obvious we are different.'

'That is why I have summoned you here today. For three sun-ups you have lived among us. Creating homes for you - albeit simple ones - was made a priority. And in his time you have yet to speak to one of our people, or make any effort to help in repairing and rebuilding. Our world is shaken, our places and our people much damaged. Are you above assisting your brethren?'

'We are above or below nothing. We have been created by the Animex with a role, sent here with a mission. This is what will be fulfilled, at the expense of everything else.'

'And what purpose is this?'

'Must you be reminded? We are here to ensure that peace is maintained, at whatever cost necessary. Your people have their task - to rebuild, to get your civilisation back on track. And we have ours.'

'So what do you do in those homes that we built?'

'We train. We ensure we are always ready for combat. We hone our skills with gun and blade. That is what we bring here that your people cannot.'

'And you will shun our society in light of that?'

The movement that Uxurus makes is too quick for Viarus to even follow. In seconds, he is gone from standing stock-still to holding the A'Nock by the throat and pressing the serrated edge of a blade into his neck.

'Shun your society? You know not of which you speak,

A'Nock. Myself and Leonis were designed for war, nothing else. While our brothers, the soldiers we trained with, go among the stars and take the fight to the enemies of the Animex, we are forced to stay here. Imagine it, Viarus. Everything you have been bred for – the only purpose you have ever had – taken away from you for *this*. A backwards society, a civilisation that can't even manage a decent war! Sitting in a hut all day, among the trees, with no challenge. Even the creatures that you fear are nothing but fodder for us. So we will not mix with you, or your society. Because you are nothing like us. We are here because it is the will of the Animex, nothing more. Rest assured, we crave to be elsewhere, *anywhere* else.'

'Please, don't...'

Uxurus shakes his head in disapproval, dropping Viarus in a heap upon the floor. A single drop of blood falls from the edge of the saw-like blade that the Noukarta still wields.

'Remember this moment, A'Nock. This is the simplest of things for us to do. We can wreak much greater destruction, wield far more force. We could have wiped out this entire settlement, but that was not what was wished of us. So do not expect camaraderie or friendship. We are here to do a duty. You stick to yours, and we will conduct ours.'

'Is that how it will be, Uxurus? The same blood in our veins, yet so little between us?'

'That is how it will be. We are here to be your warning, remember that. If there is any repeat of what happened in the clearing, then we are under strict instructions to kill all involved. There will be peace here. That is our only charge, our only commitment. Whether that threat comes from within or without, we are here and we will be ready for it.'

'What do you mean, within or without?'

Uxurus sighs, regretting his words immediately. 'Do you realise so little, Viarus? Do you think that the universe starts and ends with you? There are so many other creatures on this planet alone, let alone all of the other planets, the other stars that populate the universe! Your minds are so narrow that you cannot perceive beyond your simple homes and simple lives. There is a war raging out there, a conflict that you have never seen the likes of. Your petty squabble is nothing compared to the scale of what we have seen.'

'Will... will this war come here?'

'We do not know. But we have to be prepared if that day comes, because you cannot be. The Animex have bade it so. I have said too much already. Do not worry the rest of your people with this.'

'How can I keep such a thing secret?'

'You will keep such a thing secret or else I will have to dig deeper with my blade. Far deeper. And the same goes for any that you tell.'

Viarus shudders at the thought, but tries to maintain his calm.

'What can we do to help?'

Uxurus lets out a heavy sigh, the meaning of which Viarus cannot gauge.

'Nothing beyond what you know already. Do whatever you do. Build your civilisation. Live, thrive. That is all I can say.'

'Very well. This has been illuminating, Uxurus. I hope we have the chance to meet again.'

'The feeling is not mutual, A'Nock. Good fortune with all in Genem.'

Uxurus leads his colleague out of the house, leaving Viarus alone with his thoughts.

How much of what he needs to know was spoken, and how much was unspoken?

***

Uxurus returns to his hut, where his suit of silvered armour stands empty. He reaches into the helm, and pulls a small circular device from the very rear of it. Setting the item down on the floor, he presses a few buttons on its surface. Then he takes a seat next to it and begins to speak.

'Sejurus? Are you there?'

'Yes, Uxurus.' The voice of the Animex comes through as clear as though he was in the room itself.

'I have just met with Viarus, as you wished.'

'How did the meeting go?'

'I am not one for meetings, or discussion, my lord. I am a man of action, nothing more.'

'Still, we must be clear that you are there to co-operate.'

'We will co-operate as we see fit.'

'They are gentle creatures, Uxurus. You would do well to remember that.'

'This universe has no time for gentle creatures. They will harden up or they will die.'

'Their role is not to fight. We have other things in mind for them, greater things.'

'I see no greatness in them.'

'Give them time. Make sure there is peace, and make sure nothing interrupts their progress.'

'For that we count on you also. There is no threat here on Noukaria.'

'Of course. And I shall not let you down in that respect. I shall be watching the stars.'

'I do not understand why you have given us this assignment, but we will make sure it is done.'

'That is all I can ask of you. And be assured yours is an important role.'

'Thank you, my lord. I have training to get to.'

'Of course. Let us hope not to speak soon.'

'Indeed. Farewell, my lord.'

Uxurus hits a few more buttons on the metal disc, closing the conversation.

TO BE CONTINUED...

Lightning Source UK Ltd.
Milton Keynes UK
UKOW04f1438030715
254516UK00001B/4/P